The Amish Farmer's

Promise

A Miracle Creek Romance

Grace Springfield

ISBN 978-1-918219-82-1

First Edition: February 2026
Published by: Cosmic Jive Publishing

www.cosmicjivepublishing.com

For permissions and inquiries, contact:
info@cosmicjivepublishing.com

Disclaimer:

CHAPTER 1
The Broken Plow

The first day of October in Miracle Creek arrived not with the gentle sigh of summer's end, but with a temperamental snap in the air that spoke of winter's impatience. Susannah Mast felt it as she knelt in her herb garden behind the tidy white *daadi haus* she shared with her widowed mother. The morning sun was warm on her back, but the wind that skipped over the harvested cornfields held a blade-sharp edge, tugging at the strings of her white *kapp* and carrying the damp, melancholy scent of turned earth and decay.

At twenty-two, Susannah had a quietude about her that some in the community mistook for plainness. But those who truly knew her—who had watched her coax life back into a neighbor's failing garden, or seen the way she could calm a colicky baby with nothing more than patience and a soft song—they knew better. Her dove-gray dresses were always neat, her *kapp* always straight, her movements in church always precisely correct. But her hands, currently digging around the roots of a stubborn echinacea plant, told a different story—strong, capable, stained with soil and the green juice of herbs.

Her eyes, a clear, thoughtful gray like the sky before a snow, missed little. They were her grandmother's eyes, everyone said. Elizabeth Mast had been the district's most respected healer, a woman who could read the land like Scripture and knew the language of every growing thing. She had raised Susannah at her knee from the time she was old enough to toddle through the garden rows, teaching her which plants healed and which harmed, how to listen to what a body was trying to say through its symptoms, how to see the connections between all living things.

"The Lord made everything with a purpose, *liebling*," her *grossmammi* would say, her weathered hands sorting through bundles of dried leaves. "Our job is simply to pay attention. To watch. To listen. The answers are always there, written in root and leaf, if we have eyes to see."

Susannah had inherited those seeing eyes, along with her grandmother's gift for quietness, for making space for healing to happen. But she'd also inherited something else—a deep, bone-level loneliness that came from seeing and understanding things others couldn't quite grasp. It was as if she existed slightly apart from the world, observing it through a veil of herbs and remedies, always the helper, never quite fully participating in the life swirling around her.

"Susannah!" Her mother's voice, thin but firm, carried from the back porch. "The mending for Emma Albrecht is finished. Would you take it over before noon? She'll want to get those trousers on her *kind* before the cold sets in proper."

"*Jah, Mamm.* Right away," Susannah called back, brushing the dark loam from her hands with a practiced motion that left faint green stains on her apron. She carefully placed the echinacea root in her willow basket— it would be dried and powdered, excellent for winter ailments. The bitter, earthy scent clung to her fingers, a smell she found more comforting than any perfume.

Her mother, Ruth, leaned on the porch railing, a faded shawl around her slender shoulders. The morning light revealed what she tried to hide—the too-sharp angles of her face, the translucent quality of her skin, like paper held up to lamplight. Since *Datt*'s passing two winters ago from a sudden fever, a persistent cough had taken up residence in her chest, a ghost that refused to be banished by any of Susannah's teas or poultices. It was a silent worry that sat between them at every meal, an unwelcome third presence at their small table.

"Mind the ruts in the lane," Ruth added, her eyes soft with concern. "That last rain made a mess of it. And, Susannah?" She paused, her gaze sharpening slightly. "Veronica Zook mentioned that Barney Stoltzfus will be at the Beilers' today, helping with the barn roof. She thought you might like to know."

Susannah felt the familiar weight of expectation settle on her shoulders like a yoke. "I will be careful on the lane, Mamm," she said neutrally, deliberately addressing only the first part of her mother's statement.

Ruth's mouth tightened almost imperceptibly, but she let it pass. "Try the licorice root tea on the stove. It should soothe the tickle."

"I will," Susannah promised, lifting the basket of mending. She paused at the bottom of the porch steps, looking back at her mother's pale face, at the way she held herself too carefully, as if any sudden movement might shatter her like frost-covered glass. "Rest while I'm gone. Please, *Mamm*. The spinning can wait."

Ruth offered a faint smile that didn't quite reach her eyes. "Always doctoring. You have your *grossmammi's* hands. And her heart, I think. Always caring for everyone but yourself."

The words landed with more weight than her mother probably intended. Susannah turned away, blinking against the sudden sting in her eyes. It wasn't that she didn't care for herself. It was that she didn't quite know how, didn't know what she even wanted for herself beyond this endless cycle of tending and mending, of being needed but never quite... seen.

The walk to the Lapp farm was a tapestry of familiar

sights that usually brought her comfort. The dirt lane, hardened by the recent dry spell into a ribbon of cracked earth, wound past the Yoders' neat farmhouse with its precisely painted shutters. She greeted their new heifer, who blinked slow, liquid eyes at her over the fence, and Susannah paused to scratch the velvety space between the young cow's ears, earning a contented huff of warm, grassy breath.

Further along, she nodded to the bishop's wife, Martha, who was airing quilts in her yard, their vibrant patterns—Log Cabin, Star of Bethlehem, Wedding Ring—a defiance against the coming grey. The Bishop himself gave her a solemn nod from where he sat mending a harness on his porch, his worn hands moving with sure, timeless rhythm. His presence was like the land itself—solid, unchanging, reassuring in its permanence.

"Susannah," Martha Lapp called, her voice carrying its usual note of kindly scrutiny as she walked to the fence line, her hands still smoothing a particularly fine Double Wedding Ring quilt. "Your mother is keeping well?"

"As well as Gott allows, *denki*," Susannah replied, the practiced answer smooth on her tongue, though it tasted of dust and unspoken fears.

"And you?" Martha persisted, her sharp eyes taking in every detail of Susannah's appearance—the slight shadows under her eyes, the thinness that came from forgetting to eat when tending to others, the old-fashioned way she still wore her *kapp* strings tied beneath her chin instead of hanging loose like some of the younger women. "The singing is this Sunday evening. Barney Stoltzfus was asking after you. Again."

She let the word linger meaningfully. "His mother mentioned he's been most attentive since his father transferred the farm deed to him last month. A young man with his own land, ready to settle... it's a blessing to have such interest."

The unspoken question hung in the air, as persistent as the autumn flies. *Barney is a good man, from a good family. Why do you hesitate? What more could you want?*

"The Lord's will be done," Susannah murmured, offering a small, noncommittal smile before continuing on her way, her pulse quickening slightly with the desire to escape.

Barney *was* suitable. She could catalog his virtues like items on a shelf: Steady. Kind. From a prosperous farm with rich bottom land. His laughter came ready and easy. His family was cheerful, their home always filled with the warm chaos of visiting relatives and abundant meals. When he smiled at her across a room—and he did so often, his intentions clear as spring water—she felt nothing but a mild, friendly warmth, like the sun on a stone wall. Present, but not penetrating. Comforting, but not transforming.

It was a warmth that asked nothing of her secret self, the part that whispered to plants in the dark hours before dawn and dreamed in the language of soil and scent. The part that sometimes stood at her window on moonlit nights and felt an aching, wordless longing for something she couldn't name, something deeper and wilder than the comfortable, predictable life Barney offered.

She delivered the mending to a grateful, flustered Emma Albrecht, who was corralling three children under five and had a dusting of flour in her hair like early snow. The kitchen smelled of rising bread and boiled apples, a sweet, yeasty warmth that made Susannah's empty stomach clench with sudden hunger.

"You're a blessing, Susannah. A true blessing," Emma said, juggling the mended trousers while simultaneously blocking her youngest from climbing into the flour bin. "Tell your *Mamm* I'll bring some of my apple butter by tomorrow. The early Jonagolds made it especially sweet this year." She lowered her voice, glancing toward where masculine voices and the sound of hammering echoed from the barn. "Barney's out there, you know. Been asking about you. He's a good man, Susannah. Patient. Not every man would wait so long, you know."

"I should get back," Susannah said quickly, more quickly than was perhaps polite. *"Mamm* tires easily these days."

On her walk back, the basket now empty and light on her arm, Susannah took the longer route that skirted the edge of the King farm. She told herself it was to check on the late-blooming goldenrod in the ditch—excellent for tea, its sunny plumes a last gift before frost. She told herself she needed to gather more before the killing freeze came.

But her heart, traitorously, had its own reasons. It had been charting this course since the moment she'd seen him at the harvest service three weeks ago, a silent, solid figure standing apart, his gaze on the horizon rather than the social weave around him. Nathan King. Even his name felt different in her mind, weighted with something she couldn't quite define.

She barely knew him, really. He kept to himself, had since his father's death a year ago. Before that, old Isaac King had been the one to conduct the farm's business in town, to speak at church meetings, to represent the family at community gatherings. Nathan had always been the shadow, the silent worker in the fields, the son whose entire existence seemed consumed by the relentless demands of the land.

But Susannah's memory held other snapshots, small moments collected like pressed flowers over the years. She had seen him once, when she was perhaps sixteen, at a neighboring farm. A lamb had broken its leg, and while the other men discussed whether it should be butchered early, Nathan had quietly knelt beside the frightened creature. His hands—those large, work-roughened hands—had been surprisingly gentle as he set the tiny leg, his voice a low rumble that calmed the animal's panic. She'd watched from a distance, struck by the contrast between his imposing size and his tender care.

Another time, at a barn raising two summers ago, she'd seen him rest his forehead against his old mare's neck after a long day of lifting beams and driving nails. Just for a moment, his shoulders had sagged with weariness, his guard completely down. Then someone had called his name, and he'd straightened, the mask of stoic capability sliding back into place so quickly she'd wondered if she'd imagined that glimpse of vulnerability.

She had heard the respect in Noah Albrecht's voice when he spoke of Nathan: "Nathan King works harder than any two men, and his word is solid as stone. His father was the same, only harder. Old Isaac drove that boy like he was a piece of farm equipment. But Nathan never complained, never shirked. That farm would have failed a dozen times over without his back and his brain. Taught him that a man's character is his harvest, but forgot to teach him that a man's also allowed to have a life outside the furrows."

Now, as Susannah crested the small rise that gave a view over the King land, she saw him.

Nathan King's farm was one of the largest in the district, a sprawling patchwork of corn stubble, hayfields, and pasture rolling over gentle hills like a worn, beloved quilt. The barns were painted a deep, sober red, the fences straight and true. From a distance, it spoke of order, hard work, and a stubborn, silent pride.

But up close, Susannah could see the subtle signs of strain. The fence she stood beside needed paint. The once-vibrant flower beds his mother had tended were now overgrown with weeds. The farmyard, while clean, had a too-neat quality to it, an absence of the cheerful clutter that marked a home where life was fully lived. It was the tidiness of a man who had no time for anything but essential survival.

And there he was, in the far field.

Nathan was wrestling with a massive, horse-drawn plow that had clearly lodged itself against something unyielding. Even from this distance, Susannah could see the problem —the shear bolt on the moldboard had snapped, a common but frustrating break that would halt all work until it was replaced. The big Percherons, Ben and Bess, stood patiently in their traces, swishing their tails as if bemused by their master's struggle.

Nathan King was a man carved from the same oak as his fence posts. Twenty-eight years old, his shoulders were broad from a lifetime of farming, his hair the color of sun-bleached wheat stubble, catching the afternoon light like burnished gold. His face was all hard angles—strong jaw, high cheekbones, a straight nose that had clearly been broken at least once and set imperfectly. Under the brim of his straw hat, his eyes were a steady, watchful blue that made her think of deep water, of hidden depths.

He was not given to idle talk at singings or easy smiles at work frolics. He was a man of the land, his conversations held more with the soil and the sky than with people. Since his father's passing a year ago from a weak heart that finally gave out under decades of relentless labor, the full weight of the farm had settled on those shoulders. And he carried it with a silent, intense focus that bordered on isolation, as if he'd forgotten entirely how to be anything other than a beast of burden.

Most in the community found him distant, too serious, even a bit strange. But Susannah saw something different.

She saw the tension in his shoulders that spoke of a burden carried too long. She saw the careful way he handled his animals, the gentleness hidden beneath all that strength. She saw a man who had forgotten—or perhaps had never learned—how to rest.

As she watched, Nathan gave up trying to free the plowshare. He straightened with visible effort, his back protesting, and took off his hat. He ran a hand through his sweat-damp hair in a gesture of pure frustration that seemed to encompass far more than just a broken bolt. He looked toward the distant farmhouse, then at the sky as if calculating the hours of daylight left, and she saw his shoulders sag for just a moment before he forced them straight again.

The broken plow meant a day's work lost. In harvest season, when every hour of good weather was precious, a day was a lifetime. The weight of that loss was written in every line of his body.

Susannah's feet were moving before her mind fully consented. She knew the path through the edge of his woodlot, a shortcut to the field she'd used as a girl to hunt for blackberries. It wasn't proper, perhaps, for an unmarried woman to approach an unmarried man working alone, especially one she'd never directly spoken to beyond brief greetings at church. But she couldn't walk away.

The sight of his struggle, the tangible weight on him— it called to something deep within her. The same part that made her collect wounded birds and nurse them back to health in secret shoeboxes. The part that couldn't stand to see any creature suffering, human or otherwise. The healer's heart that her grandmother had recognized and nurtured, the gift that was both blessing and burden.

She emerged from the tree line a respectful distance away, the rustle of her dress lost in the wind. Her heart hammered against her ribs, making her voice come out smaller than she'd intended.

"Nathan?"

He turned, startled, his blue eyes widening in genuine surprise at the sight of her. For a long moment, he simply stared, as if she were an apparition conjured by his frustration. A faint flush crept up his neck beneath his summer tan, visible even in the afternoon light.

"Susannah." He said her name carefully, precisely, as if it were an unfamiliar tool he was learning to handle. His voice was deeper than she remembered from their brief exchanges at church, rough with disuse, like a gate hinge needing oil. "Is... is something wrong? Your mother...?"

The fact that he knew to ask about her mother first, that he'd noticed her constant care, made something warm unfold in her chest.

"No, Mamm is well… I saw from the lane. The plow. The shear bolt?" She gestured, her own voice quieter than she intended, suddenly hyperaware of the intimacy of this moment—just the two of them in this vast, open field, with nothing but the wind and the patient horses as witnesses.

"*Jah*," he said, the word a soft explosion of breath. He glanced back at the immobilized implement as if it had personally betrayed him. "Snapped clean. Metal fatigue, probably. I have spares in the workshop, but..." He looked at the horses, then at the distant barn, a quarter-mile trek across the uneven field. "It's a walk. And I'd have to unhitch them, lead them back, then come all the way out here again with the part. It'll be dark before I can get back to work."

The frustration in his voice was palpable, but underneath it, she heard something else. Exhaustion. The bone-deep weariness of a man who never allowed himself to rest, who drove himself as mercilessly as his father had once driven him.

"I could hold the team," Susannah offered quietly, taking a small step closer. The earth was cool and firm under her feet. "While you fetch it. If you'd like. They look calm." She gestured to Ben and Bess, who swiveled their massive ears toward her voice, their dark eyes gentle and curious.

He stared at her for a long moment, his expression unreadable. The offer was practical, helpful, the sort of neighborly gesture that happened every day in a close-knit community. But in Miracle Creek, where every interaction between unmarried men and women was watched and weighed and discussed over quilting frames and in workshop corners, such an offer was also a thread crossing the careful weave of propriety.

Accepting her help would tie them together, however briefly, in the community's watchful eyes. She saw the calculation in his gaze—the desperate need for efficiency warring with a lifetime of solitary discipline, of careful distance from anything that might distract him from his duty to the land.

Finally, he gave a single, curt nod. "That would be... a kindness. A great kindness. *Denki*." The gratitude in his voice was so genuine, so unguarded, that it struck her like a physical touch.

He moved closer to show her how to hold the lines, and Susannah's breath caught. This close, she could see the fine lines at the corners of his eyes from squinting into the sun, the small scar above his left eyebrow, the exact shade of blue in his irises—not a flat, simple color, but layered, like looking through clear water to stones and sky beneath. She could smell the honest scent of his labor—clean sweat, sun-warmed cotton, and underneath it all, something earthier. Soil and growing things. The smell of a man who was part of the land he worked.

His calloused fingers brushed against hers as he transferred the leather reins, and a spark—simple and shocking—leapt between them.

It was not metaphorical. It was a jolt of pure awareness, a current that ran from her fingertips to the core of her, lighting up parts of herself she hadn't known existed. Her whole body seemed to wake up, every nerve suddenly alive and singing.

He pulled his hand back as if stung, his eyes flying to hers. In that fleeting contact, she saw not just surprise, but a mirror of her own sudden, breathless awareness. His eyes, she realized in that electric moment, were not just blue, but the exact color of the chicory flowers that bloomed by the roadside in high summer—bright and startling against the mundane dust of everyday life.

"Just... keep a steady pressure," he muttered, not meeting her eyes now, his focus suddenly, intensely on the horizon. "They know the drill. They're good horses. My father trained them, and they've been working these fields for eight years. They won't bolt or spook." He was talking too much, she realized. Filling the charged air with words that didn't matter.

Then he was striding away toward the barn, his long legs eating up the distance, his retreating back straight as one of his fence posts. But there was something in the set of his shoulders, a tension that hadn't been there before, that told her she wasn't the only one affected by that touch.

Alone in the vast, silent field with the sighing wind and the patient horses, Susannah's heart hammered against her ribs like a trapped bird testing the bars of its cage. The touch had been nothing—an accidental brush of skin that happened dozens of times a day in the ordinary course of life. And yet it was everything. It was the first crack in the quiet shell of her world, letting in a light she hadn't known was missing, showing her a landscape of possibility she'd never imagined existed.

She spoke softly to the horses in Pennsylvania Dutch, the old words comforting them—and herself. "*Sei still, mei Schätzli. Alles ist gut.*" Be still, my treasures. All is well.

Ben turned his massive head to regard her with one liquid dark eye, then blew out a contented breath that ruffled his velvet nose. Bess shifted her weight, her harness creaking comfortably, and leaned just slightly toward Susannah's presence, seeking the comfort of human contact.

As she waited, she looked out over Nathan King's land. It was beautiful in its austere, autumn way, all muted golds and browns under the vast bowl of the sky. The harvested cornfield rolled away in neat, parallel rows of stubble. In the distance, she could see the dark green squares of winter wheat already sprouting, the promise of next year's bread already being written in the soil. Further still, the wooded hills that marked the edge of the district rose like gentle waves frozen in time.

But it was also a weight, she realized. A responsibility that allowed no rest, no space for anything but endless labor. She thought of Nathan's solitary figure against the sky, of the careful distance he kept from the community, of the way he'd looked at the failing light with something close to despair. And a strange, protective ache settled in her chest, an emotion both new and instantly familiar, as if it had been waiting there all along for the right moment to wake.

* * *

He returned quicker than she expected, a new bolt and a heavy wrench in hand. He worked with efficient, practiced motions, not speaking, the muscles in his forearms corded with effort. She watched the play of strength and skill, the way he handled the heavy tool with the same gentleness he'd shown the lamb years ago. Everything he did, she realized, he did with care, even when no one was watching.

The silence between them was no longer empty, but charged, thick with things unsaid, with the memory of that spark. When the new bolt was secured and the plow freed with a satisfying groan of metal, he stood and took the lines from her. Their hands did not touch this time; he was careful, deliberate in his distance.

But the current was still there, humming in the air between them like the afternoon heat rising from the turned earth.

"*Denki,*" he said again, his voice low, meant for her alone in the wide field. His gaze held hers, and the intensity in his blue eyes was like a physical touch— searching, questioning, hoping. "I... I am in your debt."

"Ach, I was nothing," she whispered, finding her voice with effort. "Just... neighbors helping neighbors."

He nodded slowly, as if tasting the word, testing its weight and finding it somehow insufficient. "Neighbors," he repeated. Then, hesitantly, as if each word were a stone he was placing with great care, building something fragile and precious, he added, "The... the apple harvest is next week. Thursday. We press cider that day. The early Russets and the late Romes together. If... if you and your *mamm* would have need of some. For your cellar. For the winter."

It wasn't an invitation to a singing. It wasn't a declaration or a proposal. It was a farmer offering the fruits of his labor, the simplest, most honest gift he knew how to give. But in the intricate, unspoken language of Miracle Creek, where courtship moved as slowly and deliberately as the seasons, where every gesture carried weight and meaning, it was as bold as a shout across the fields.

It was an opening. A possibility. A door left carefully, purposefully ajar.

Susannah felt a smile touch her lips, genuine and unforced, warming her from within like sunlight breaking through clouds. "We would like that very much. *Denki*, Nathan. That's very kind."

She turned to leave, and felt his eyes on her back all the way to the tree line, a sensation as sure and tangible as sunlight on her shoulders. The wind was colder now, cutting through her dress, but she didn't feel it. A new warmth, fragile and terrifying and impossibly precious, had taken root inside her—a seedling of hope in fallow ground, tender and green and reaching toward light she hadn't known she needed.

* * *

Nathan King watched Susannah Mast disappear into the woods, her gray dress blending with the shadows until she was gone, like a dream dispersing in daylight. He stood motionless for a long moment, the leather lines slack in his hands, the horses shifting restlessly behind him, wondering why they hadn't moved.

The familiar weight of his responsibilities—the broken plow now fixed, the endless acres still to be worked before winter, the echoing silence of the big, empty farmhouse waiting for him at day's end—felt suddenly different. Not lighter, exactly. The weight was still there, solid and unchanging as the land itself. But shared, somehow. Witnessed.

For the first time since his father died, someone had stepped into his field, into his struggle, without being asked. Without expectation of payment or favor. She had simply *seen* him—not the capable farmer, not Isaac King's son and heir, not the valuable workhorse the community depended on—but him. A man. Struggling. Alone.

And she had offered help without pity, without judgment. Just quiet, capable assistance, as natural as breathing. It was the Amish way but there was something about her service that had touched him more.

He looked down at his hand, the one she'd touched. He could still feel the ghost of her touch, a tingling memory on his work-roughened skin that seemed to have burned itself into his very bones. When was the last time someone had touched him with gentleness? When was the last time a touch had meant anything other than a handshake after church or a slap on the back during a barn raising?

Her hands had been smaller than his, the skin soft despite her work, stained faintly green from whatever herbs she'd been handling. Healer's hands. His father would have dismissed such things as foolish women's work, inferior to real doctoring. The kind of thing Davi Mathews did. But Nathan had seen Susannah's skill firsthand last spring, when Jacob Yoder's prize cow had developed a udder infection that threatened to turn septic. The *Englisch* vet had been away, and Jacob had been beside himself.

Susannah had appeared quietly, summoned by someone, and had spent an hour in that barn. She'd emerged with a poultice of something—mullein, he'd heard later—that she'd gathered from the damp spot by the creek. Within two days, the cow had turned the corner. Within a week, she was fully healed. Abner had tried to pay Susannah, but she'd refused, accepting only a jar of his wife's strawberry preserves.

"Just neighbors," she'd said then too.

Nathan had been in the barn that day, helping Abner with other chores. He'd watched her work from a distance, had seen the calm confidence in her movements, the way she'd spoken to the suffering animal in low, soothing Pennsylvania Dutch. He'd seen something else too—a deep, almost spiritual connection to the work of healing, as if she were partnering with forces beyond human understanding.

She'd been seventeen then, still a girl really, though already carrying herself with the quiet competence of a woman. He'd been twenty-three, newly aware of the growing weight of his father's expectations, of the narrowing path his life was taking. He'd noticed her briefly, the way a man notices a particularly lovely sunset—with appreciation but no thought that such beauty had anything to do with his own daily reality.

But over the years, he'd noticed her more. Always from a distance, always in glimpses. The way she moved through the community like a quiet stream, nourishing everything she touched. The shadows under her eyes that spoke of late nights tending to her mother. The genuine kindness in her face when she spoke with *kinner*, never condescending, always respectful. The way she stood slightly apart at gatherings, observing, her gray eyes missing nothing.

He'd never allowed himself to think beyond those observations. What was the point? His *datt* had made it clear: the farm came first, last, and always. There was no time for courting, for the slow dance of relationship building. There was only work, endless work, the kind that ground a man down to his essential elements and then demanded more.

But his *datt* was gone now. The farm was his, to manage as he saw fit. The old man's ghost still haunted the fields, yes, whispering criticisms in every creaking board and overgrown fence line. But it was just a ghost. The living man, with his iron will and his impossible standards, was gone.

And in his place was this strange, terrifying sense of possibility. This question that had been growing in Nathan's mind for months now, crystallizing in the moment Susannah Mast's fingers had brushed his: *What if there's more to life than this endless cycle of planting and harvest?*

What if a man could have both—the land he loves and someone to share it with? What if this crushing loneliness isn't the price of faithfulness, but a sign that something's missing?

He looked toward the west pasture, the one his father had always called a lost cause. Rocky, poor soil, eternally troublesome. A cross to bear. But Nathan had been reading the agricultural pamphlets David Mathews passed along, had been thinking thoughts his father would have called newfangled nonsense. Clover to fix nitrogen. Fruit trees for windbreaks and extra income. Not fighting the land's nature, but working with it.

It could be more than it was. It could be abundant instead of merely enduring. But it would take years of patient work. And help. It wasn't one-man work, not if it was to be done right.

"Slow work is better shared," his own father had said once, in a rare moment of philosophy. He'd been talking about building a stone wall, but the principle held.

Nathan picked up the reins, clicked to the team. "Come on, you two," he murmured, his voice rough. "Daylight's wasting."

But as the plow bit back into the earth, cutting a straight, dark furrow through the stubble, Nathan's thoughts were not on the depth of the cut or the yield to come. They were on a pair of clear gray eyes that saw more than most. On small, capable hands stained with the green of growing things. On a voice that gentled frightened animals and probably gentled frightened hearts just as easily.

And on the sweet, promised taste of cider on Thursday —an excuse, a beginning, a carefully placed stone in a foundation he was only now realizing he wanted to build.

* * *

The sun was setting as he finally led the team back to the barn, painting the sky in shades of amber and rose. He paused in the barnyard, looking toward where he knew the Mast farm lay beyond the rise of land, though he couldn't see it from here. Somewhere over there, Susannah was probably tending to her mother, preparing supper, moving through her evening routine with the same quiet grace she brought to everything.

Did she feel it too? That spark? Or had it been only him, a lonely man reading meaning into a simple touch?

He thought he's seen it in her eyes. Thursday would tell. Thursday, with its cider pressing and its community gathering and its legitimate excuse to see if those gray eyes would seek his across a crowded farmyard. Thursday, when he would offer not just cider, but the first tentative threads of something more, if she would accept them.

For the first time in longer than he could remember, Nathan King went to bed that night with something other than exhaustion pulling him toward sleep. He lay in the darkness of his lonely room and felt, against all reason and experience, a fragile, dangerous thing uncurling in his chest.

Hope. And his heart praised Gott for it.

CHAPTER 2
The Cider Pressing

Thursday dawned clear and cold, the frost laying a crisp, silver veil over the stubbled fields, etching each blade of grass in crystalline detail. The promise of cider pressing hung in the air, a communal ritual that marked the turning of the season from harvest to hearth, from outward labor to inward gathering. For Susannah, the day carried a nervous undercurrent, a flutter in her stomach that had nothing to do with the sharp weather. It felt like the morning of a church communion, charged with a silent significance that made her hands tremble slightly as she braided her blonde hair before the small mirror in her room.

She had woken before dawn, unable to sleep, her mind turning over the memory of Nathan's words by the broken plow. *The apple harvest is next week. We press cider on Thursday. If you and your mamm would have need of some.* Such simple words, spoken in that rough, careful voice of his. But they had echoed in her thoughts every night since, a promise as tangible as the apple he'd given her, which still sat on her windowsill, its skin now slightly wrinkled but still fragrant, still beautiful. She couldn't bring herself to eat it or throw it away. It had become a talisman, a physical anchor to that moment in the field when something fundamental had shifted between them.

Her mother, Ruth, had raised a thin, questioning eyebrow that morning when Susannah mentioned the King cider pressing while packing a basket with jars of her mother's famous chow-chow—the tangy, colorful relish of cabbage, peppers, and beans that was always in demand—and a loaf of fragrant rye bread, still warm from the early morning baking.

"Nathan King himself invited us?" Ruth asked, her voice layered with gentle surprise. She set down her teacup with a soft *clink* against the saucer, her pale eyes studying her daughter's face with a mother's acute perception. "Not through his aunt Edna, or through word passed at church, but directly?"

"*Jah, Mamm.* When I helped with his plow." Susannah kept her voice even, focusing intently on tucking a checkered cloth around the bread to keep it warm, her fingers smoothing the fabric with perhaps more care than was strictly necessary.

"A kind gesture," Ruth said, her tone careful as she sipped her tea, the steam rising between them like a veil. She coughed softly, a dry sound that seemed to scrape the quiet of the kitchen, a reminder of her fragility. "He is a man with a heavy load. Not one for society. Prefers the company of his trees and his livestock, they say."

She paused, watching Susannah's reaction. "But his apples..." A faint smile touched her lips, softening the concern in her eyes. "His apples are always the sweetest in the district. His mother had a gift for grafting. She could make even the sourest rootstock produce fruit that tasted like honey."

It was both an approval and a gentle warning, coded in the way of Plain mothers who did not speak directly of courtship but conveyed volumes through observation. Nathan's solitude was noted, a fact as plain as the black buggies on a Sunday road. But his mother's legacy—that gift for nurturing sweetness from difficult stock—that was noted too.

Susannah felt her cheeks warm despite the cool kitchen air. "He works hard," she said quietly, carefully arranging jars in the basket. "The farm is his whole world."

"And what world would be yours, in such a life?" Ruth asked, not unkindly, but with the penetrating directness born of love and worry. "A woman needs more than a well-run farm, Susannah. She needs a companion. Someone who sees her, not just the work her hands can do."

Susannah thought of Nathan's eyes when he'd looked at her across that field—not with casual interest or the appraising gaze she'd felt from others, but with something deeper. Recognition. As if he'd found something he hadn't known he was searching for.

"I think," she said slowly, meeting her mother's gaze, "he sees more than most people realize. He just... shows it differently."

Ruth studied her daughter for a long moment, then nodded, a slight movement that held resignation and blessing in equal measure. "Then we shall go. And we shall see what we see."

* * *

The King farmyard, when they arrived mid-morning, was a scene of ordered industry and cheerful chaos that seemed to pulse with communal energy. A large, old-fashioned wooden cider press, its timbers darkened by decades of use and stained with the memory of countless harvests, stood in the center like an altar. Its massive screw and slatted baskets were ready for the sacrament of fruit. The morning sun caught the metal bands that held it together, making them gleam like silver.

Already, several families were there—Susannah saw Emma and Noah Albrecht near the press, Noah explaining something about the mechanism to their curious oldest boy, who stared with wide, wonder-filled eyes at the enormous contraption, his small hand clutching his father's leg. Eli Fisher was hefting bushel baskets with his brother-in-law, Barney Stoltzfus, their laughter ringing out across the yard, warm and masculine and easy. Deborah Peachey-Lapp chatted with Charity Beiler near a trestle table being laden with pies, breads, and smoked meats, their voices creating a comfortable murmur of domesticity. The whole scene was painted in the gold and amber tones of autumn, the air sharp and clean and scented with apples.

And there was Nathan, at the heart of it all yet somehow apart, like a solitary oak in a meadow. He was directing the unloading of a wagon heaped with a small mountain of apples—a fragrant mix of ruby-red Romes and golden-green Russets that shone like jewels in the pale sun, each variety carefully separated. He moved with a quiet authority, nodding instructions, catching a basket a younger boy—one of the Beiler sons—nearly fumbled with one easy, sure hand, steadying it without rebuke or fuss.

When he saw Susannah and her mother approaching, he paused mid-sentence to the boy, his hand still on the basket. For a moment, his serious expression softened into something akin to relief, a subtle light kindling in his blue eyes like the first stars appearing in a twilight sky, as if he'd been waiting for a sign and it had just arrived. His shoulders, which had been held with tension, seemed to ease just slightly.

"Ruth. Susannah," he said, meeting them halfway across the yard. His boots crunched on the frost-hardened ground. His words were simple, but he held Susannah's gaze a beat longer than propriety strictly required, long enough that she felt the warmth rise in her cheeks. "Welcome. The press is ready."

He took the basket from Susannah, his fingers brushing the woven handle where hers had been, a deliberate echo of their first touch. She felt it like a spark traveling up her arm.

"Your bread," he said, glancing into the basket, "and your *mamm's* chow-chow. The table will groan under such weight. *Denki* for this. The table is over there with the others."

"A fine yield, Nathan," Ruth said, her keen eyes taking in the mountains of apples, the bustling activity, the evidence of careful planning and hard work. "Your father would be proud. And your mother—this many apples speaks to her care of those trees, still bearing fruit years after her hands last touched them."

"*Gott's* blessing," he replied simply, a standard phrase, but he gave a slight, acknowledging nod that seemed to carry genuine gratitude. His jaw worked slightly, as if he wanted to say more but couldn't find the words. Then, as Ruth was led toward the table by Martha Lapp, who immediately began fussing over her and finding her a comfortable seat on a bench in the sun, he turned his body slightly toward Susannah, his voice dropping to a pitch meant for her alone, intimate despite the crowd.

"The goldenrods by the ditch where you were... they're still blooming. Just a few. The late ones that survived the first frost." He gestured vaguely toward the road, his eyes never leaving hers. "If you had need of more for your teas. The ones that survive the frost are stronger, you said."

He remembered. Not just her, but the specific, mundane reason she'd given for being on that road. The detail of it, the specificity, the fact that he'd noticed what still bloomed even as he managed a farm and a pressing— the observation sent a wave of warmth through her, more potent than any stove-heat, flooding from her chest outward to her fingertips.

"I gathered enough for the winter," she said softly, her voice barely carrying over the cheerful noise of the gathering. Then, daring a little more, she added, "But I will watch them. The last flowers often hold the strongest medicine. They've survived more than the others. There's a... a resilience in them that's valuable."

It was the wisdom of generations, not learnt from any book.

He held her gaze, a silent understanding passing between them, a conversation happening beneath the words about much more than goldenrod. His eyes seemed to search hers, looking for something, finding it. "*Jah*," he said finally, his voice rough with an emotion he couldn't quite name. "They do. The strongest medicine comes from the plants that have weathered the most."

The moment stretched, gossamer-thin and precious, before the sound of Eli Fisher's hearty laugh shattered it. "Nathan! These Romes aren't going to grind themselves! Come show this youngling how to work the crusher before he grinds his fingers along with the apples!"

Nathan's gaze held Susannah's for one more heartbeat, reluctant to break the connection, then he nodded once—a small, private acknowledgment—and turned back to his duties.

* * *

The work began in earnest, a symphony of purposeful noise and coordinated movement. The women and older girls sorted and washed apples at long tubs of cold water, their laughter and chatter weaving through the yard like a bright thread. The men and boys took turns grinding the apples into pomace in the hand-cranked crusher, the sharp, sweet, almost intoxicating scent of crushed fruit filling the air, tangy and irresistible, making mouths water. Then the fragrant pomace was layered into the press's cloth-lined baskets with practiced efficiency, and the great wooden screw was turned, slowly, steadily, by strong arms. The first golden juice trickled, then streamed into waiting buckets, a liquid harvest that caught the sunlight and seemed to glow.

Susannah found herself working beside Sarah Mathews at the washing tubs, her hands plunged into the cold water, the shock of it making her fingers ache. Sarah, her face rosy from the cool air and steam rising from the warmer washing water, gave her a knowing, kind look as she passed a basket of apples, their surfaces still dusty from the orchard floor.

"I saw you helping Nathan with his plow the other day," she said quietly, her hands never stopping their efficient work, turning each apple to check for damage before dropping it into the clean water with a soft *plunk*. "Barney came home and said a broken shear bolt can try a man's patience on a tight schedule. Said Nathan looked like he was arguing with the earth itself, and the earth was winning."

"It seemed the neighborly thing for me to do," Susannah said, feeling her cheeks heat despite the cool water numbing her hands. She focused intently on scrubbing a particularly dirty apple. "Anyone would have done the same."

"Neighborly," Sarah echoed, her hazel eyes twinkling with a wisdom born of her own love story with David Mathews, an *Englischer doktor* who had chosen her and her world at great cost. "*Jah*. It's often how it starts. With a small kindness. A hand offered when it's needed most."

Her glance drifted to where David was now manning the press handle with Eli, the two men—one Plain, one not—working in easy, powerful unison, their different worlds brought together by love and respect. The muscles in their forearms stood out like cords as they turned the massive screw, the juice flowing faster.

There was a whole history in Sarah's look, a story of fences mended and storms weathered, of a love that had patiently bridged two worlds and in doing so, changed both. Susannah felt a sudden, fierce longing for a connection that profound, that transformative. Something that would make her feel truly, completely *known*.

Sarah's voice softened further, barely audible over the splash of water. "You have a good heart, Susannah. A careful heart. But don't be *too* careful. Sometimes the safest choice is just the one that looks safe from a distance. Up close, it can be just as uncertain."

She squeezed Susannah's wet hand briefly, warmly. "Follow the pull. Trust that feeling in your chest when you look at him. That recognition. It's much rarer than people think."

Before Susannah could respond, Veronica Zook appeared at her elbow with an empty basket. "Susannah, dear, would you be so kind as to carry this fresh bushel to the grinding station? Young Isaiah has his hands full." The older woman's eyes were sharp despite her smile, clearly having noted the intimate conversation.

* * *

As the morning wore on, Susannah felt Nathan's gaze like a tangible thing, a warm spot between her shoulder blades, a gentle pressure that made her hyper-aware of every movement. When she carried a bucket of peelings to the compost heap at the edge of the yard, she looked up to find him watching her from across the busy space, a bushel basket balanced on his hip, his expression unreadable but intent. The world seemed to narrow to just that line of sight between them. Her breath caught.

When he brought a fresh bushel to her washing station, their hands met briefly in the transfer of the heavy basket, his rough, capable fingers sliding against hers for just a moment longer than necessary. His were cold from handling the fruit, hers warm from the water. The contrast sent a shiver through her that had nothing to do with temperature.

"You work hard," he murmured, his voice a low rumble near her ear as he leaned in, close enough that she could smell the clean scent of him—soap, and hay, and autumn air. Close enough to see the fine lines at the corners of his eyes, earned from squinting into sun over distant fields.

"As do you," she replied, daring to meet his eyes, finding herself momentarily lost in their blue depth. She saw not just the fatigue of a man who rose before dawn every day of his life, but a flicker of the same loneliness that sometimes echoed in her own quiet hours—the loneliness of the caregiver, the solitary steward who carried weight that others couldn't see.

The moment broke as someone called for more apples, but the connection lingered like a held breath.

* * *

The cider flowed, golden and fragrant, into gleaming buckets and jars. The first, fresh cup was always offered to the elders and the children—tradition and blessing. Susannah took a cup to her mother, who sat on a bench wrapped in her shawl, talking with Esther Coblentz, their grey heads bent together in that way of women who had known each other since childhood. Ruth's face had more color than it had in weeks, the pleasure of community as healing as any of Susannah's remedies.

As Susannah turned from them, adjusting her shawl against a sudden gust of wind, she nearly collided with a solid form. Strong hands caught her elbows, steadying her.

"Susannah!" Barney Stoltzfus said, his pleasant, open face breaking into an easy smile as he released her, stepping back a respectful distance. He was a handsome man in the conventional way—his build solid and capable, his features even, his temperament as predictable and even as a well-kept pasture in summer. "A good day for it, *jah*? Crisp air, sweet apples. The Kings always have the best pressings."

He fell into step beside her as she moved to return to her work, his presence comfortable and expected, like a familiar hymn. "I was hoping to see you at the singing last Sunday. Saved a bench near the back, where it's quiet. Away from the younger ones and their carrying-on."

"*Mamm* wasn't feeling well," she said, which was true, though not the whole truth. The whole truth was a lack of a pull, an absence of the nervous anticipation she felt standing here now, her heart still beating faster from those brief seconds near Nathan. With Barney, there was only a mild, friendly warmth, like the sun on a stone wall— present, but not penetrating. It was a warmth that asked nothing of her secret self, the part that whispered to plants and dreamed in the language of soil and scent.

"I'm sorry to hear it. She looks better today, though. The fresh air and fellowship." He smiled at her, his brown eyes earnest. "Perhaps this Sunday? The singing is at the Lapps'. They have that big barn, plenty of room. And Martha always makes the best butter cookies."

Before she could form a noncommittal answer, practice in the art of gentle deflection, a raised voice—a man's sharp command—cut through the communal hum like a knife. "Whoa, now! Easy, easy!"

One of the older King horses, a massive draft gelding named Major with a coat like burnished copper, tied near the equipment shed, had suddenly thrown his head up, snorting in alarm and pawing the ground with increasing agitation, his iron-shod hoof striking sparks from a stone embedded in the packed earth. His eyes rolled white, showing the whites, and his enormous body tensed with fear.

"Whoa, now! Easy!" Nathan was there in an instant, moving faster than Susannah had ever seen him move, his hand reaching for the horse's sweaty neck, speaking in low, steady Pennsylvania Dutch, the old, soothing words. "*Sei ruhig, alter Freund. Sei ruhig.*"

But the horse was spooked, caught in his panic, rolling his eyes white and tossing his massive head with enough force to snap a man's arm.

"He's twisted his hoof in that tarp strap," John Hostetler observed grimly, pointing to where a corner of a canvas tarpaulin had blown loose from a pile of equipment and tangled tightly around the horse's pastern, the thick strap wrapping like a snare. Each movement the horse made pulled it tighter.

Nathan knelt in the dirt without hesitation, his big hands careful but firm as he tried to loosen the stiff, unyielding canvas, working the knot with practiced fingers. But the horse, anxiety mounting with each passing second, shifted its immense weight, its hip bumping Nathan hard and sending him sprawling backward into the damp, cold earth with a solid *thud* that knocked the breath from his lungs.

A collective gasp went up from the women nearby. Veronica Zook clutched her apron to her chest. Emma Albrecht's hand flew to her mouth. Barney took a step forward, then hesitated, his face uncertain—wanting to help but not knowing how to approach a frightened animal of that size.

Susannah didn't think. Her body moved on an instinct older than propriety, older than the careful walls she'd built around her own heart. She was at Nathan's side in moments, kneeling beside him in the dirt, heedless of her good dress, heedless of the watching eyes. "Are you hurt?"

He shook his head, more embarrassed than injured, she could see that immediately. A smear of rich, dark soil streaked his cheekbone, and there would be bruises tomorrow, but his eyes were clear. His focus was entirely on the frightened animal. "He'll pull if he gets more scared," Nathan said, his voice tight with urgency. "Could break his leg or the post. Or hurt someone."

"Let me," she said, the words calm and sure, spoken with the authority she used in her healing work. Without waiting for permission, she moved toward the horse's head, positioning herself carefully in its line of sight, a small, gray figure before the towering beast. She didn't reach immediately for the tangled leg. Instead, she began to speak, not in English, but in the same soft, rhythmic Dutch Nathan had used, the language of their childhood and their deepest selves, the language of prayer and lullaby.

"*Sei still, alter Freund. Alles ist gut. Wir helfen dir. Sei still.*" Be still, old friend. All is well. We will help you. Be still.

Her voice was a calm stream, a balm on raw nerves. She held out her open hand, palm up, non-threatening, letting the horse blow his warm, grassy breath against her skin, letting him smell her—earth and herbs and no threat. His rolling eye fixed on her, drawn by the unwavering calm in her voice, and the terrible tension in his massive neck eased just a fraction, a shudder running through his flesh like wind through grass.

"Now," she murmured to Nathan, not taking her eyes off the horse's deep, liquid gaze, maintaining that fragile connection. "Slowly."

Nathan, still on the ground, swiftly but carefully untwisted the canvas, his strong fingers working the knot with the skill born of a lifetime of such work, freeing the pastern with a final, sharp pull. The strap fell away, harmless now. The horse let out a great, shuddering sigh, his head lowering, his weight settling back onto all four hooves. The crisis passed like a storm cloud moving on, leaving only trembling aftermath.

Nathan stood slowly, brushing dirt from his trousers with hands that shook slightly—not from fear, but from the adrenaline draining away. He looked from the calmed animal, now nuzzling Susannah's shoulder in thanks, a gentle giant once more, to Susannah herself.

His expression was one of open astonishment and a deep, unfeigned admiration that made her heart turn over completely in her chest. "You have a way," he said, the words full of a respect that went far deeper than courtesy or social nicety. It was the recognition of a fellow craftsperson, one who spoke a language he understood— the language of care, of patience, of seeing fear and meeting it with steady calm. "A way with frightened creatures. With... with the wild parts that fear the harness."

The words seemed to carry layers of meaning, speaking about more than just the horse.

Barney Stoltzfus, who had watched the whole scene from a few feet away, now stepped forward, offering a jovial, "Well done, both of you! That could have been a real tragedy!" But his smile seemed a little tight, a little forced, not quite reaching his eyes as it usually did. The moment of unspoken, intimate collaboration between Susannah and Nathan—the shared language, the seamless trust, the way they had worked as one mind in two bodies —had been obvious to all.

It had drawn a line in the farmyard dust, clear as a fence, and Barney found himself on the other side of it. His jaw tightened almost imperceptibly.

* * *

The rest of the afternoon passed in a blur for Susannah, her senses heightened to an almost unbearable degree. She was acutely aware of Nathan's presence as if he were a magnet and she were iron filings, feeling a pull toward him as tangible as gravity, as undeniable as the turn of seasons. When he laughed at something John Hostetler said—a rare, genuine sound that transformed his whole face—she felt it in her chest like a bell ringing. When he moved past her to fetch another basket, the space between them seemed to hum with awareness.

As the sun began its descent and the shadows lengthened, painting the yard in long bars of gold and amber, families began to prepare for departure. The cider had been divided, each family receiving their share in repurposed milk jars and mason jars, the liquid treasure carefully apportioned. The children were wound down from their sugar and excitement, becoming quiet and clingy.

When it came time for Susannah and Ruth to leave, Nathan filled two gallon jars with the clear, amber cider—the finest of the pressing, from the first, purest flow—and brought them to their buggy himself, his boots crunching on the frost-hardened ground.

"For your mother," he said, handing them carefully to Ruth, who sat wrapped in blankets on the buggy seat, looking tired but content. "The first pressing. The sweetest."

"You are generous, Nathan," Ruth said warmly, genuine affection in her voice. "Too generous. This is your hard work."

"It's shared work," he replied simply. "Shared labor, shared harvest. That's the way."

Then he turned to Susannah, and from his coat pocket —not from the communal supply, but from somewhere he'd kept it separate and safe—he produced a single, perfect Russet apple. Its skin was blushed with pink where the sun had kissed it most devotedly, its stem small and neat, and it seemed to glow in the fading light as if lit from within.

"And this," he said, his voice so low it was almost lost in the crunch of departing buggy wheels and the calls of farewell, meant only for her ears, "for the one who calms troubled creatures. For the one who sees the fear beneath the fight."

Their fingers touched as she took the apple, cool and smooth and perfect. This time, the spark was not a shock, but a slow burn, a warmth that started where their skin met and spread through her entire body, settling somewhere deep in her chest, a promise that warmed her from the inside out.

"*Denki*, Nathan," she whispered, cradling the fruit like a treasure, like something precious and fragile that must be protected.

He held her gaze for a heartbeat longer than was strictly proper, the world narrowing to the space between them, to the shared breath, to the unspoken promise hanging in the cooling air. The sounds of the departing crowd faded. There was only him, and her, and this moment that felt suspended outside of time.

"The fence along the west pasture needs mending next week," he said suddenly, the words abrupt, practical, but his eyes told a different story. "The posts are rotten, and the ground is rocky. Stubborn work. It's slow work. For one."

It wasn't an invitation, not in the traditional sense. It was a statement of fact, plain as day, as straightforward as the man himself. But the meaning was as clear as the autumn air, a question asked in the language of labor and partnership. *Will you come?*

Susannah felt a smile bloom from deep within, a feeling like the first green shoot breaking through frozen ground in spring, like sap rising in a tree after winter's death. "Slow work is better shared," she said softly, meeting his challenging gaze with one of her own, accepting what he offered—not just help with a fence, but something far more profound. "One set of hands gets tired. Two sets can spell each other. Can steady the posts while the other packs the earth."

A nod, almost imperceptible, but his eyes lit from within, a spark catching and blazing into something steady and warm. "*Jah*," he agreed, the word final, a covenant sealed. "It is. Much better shared."

He stepped back, releasing her from that intense gaze, and she felt the loss of it like a physical thing. But the promise remained, solid and real between them.

* * *

On the ride home, the rhythmic clip-clop of the horse a soothing cadence, the buggy swaying gently, Ruth was quiet for a long time. The jars of cider sat cradled in her lap like sleeping infants, catching the last rays of the setting sun over Miracle Creek. The world was painted in shades of purple and deep blue, the first stars beginning to appear in the darkening sky.

Finally, as their own farm came into view, the familiar shapes of barn and house black silhouettes against the twilight, she spoke, her voice measured, each word chosen with care.

"Nathan King is a *gut* man. A righteous man. I knew his father, Isaac—stubborn as an oak, faithful as the sunrise, hard as iron but with a soft heart for his family. Nathan is cast from the same mold." She paused, coughing softly. "But his life *is* his farm, Susannah. It is his first love and his last duty. It leaves little room for... else. For frivolity. For an easy breath. For idle afternoons or spontaneous joy. The land demands everything, and he gives it."

"I know, *Mamm*," Susannah said, looking down at the perfect apple in her hand, its clean, sharp scent filling the buggy, mixing with the sweeter perfume of the cider. She turned it slowly, watching how the last light caught on its skin.

"And Barney Stoltzfus asks for you," her mother continued gently, not looking at her daughter but straight ahead at the road. "His life would be... easier. Lighter on the heart. His family is cheerful. There is laughter in that house, music, ease. His mother told me he's already building an addition to the house, planning for a family. He's a man who looks forward with hope, not backward with duty. That kind of sunshine... it's not a small thing, Susannah."

Susannah thought of Nathan's steady blue eyes, like a deep well holding quiet strength and hidden depths. She thought of the weight of his responsibility, which he wore not as a complaint but as a harness—something that allowed him to pull his load, to be useful, to fulfill his purpose. She thought of the silent, growing language they were beginning to share, built on glances and deeds and a recognition that went soul-deep, more eloquent than any flattery or easy words.

She thought of Barney's easy smile, his pleasant conversation that washed over her like water over stone—present, but leaving no mark. His cheerfulness that left her soul unmoved, untouched, like a calm, shallow pond. Safe, yes. But not alive with hidden currents.

"The heart has its own geography, *Mamm*," she said quietly, echoing something Esther Coblentz had told her years ago, when Susannah was just a girl nursing a fledgling sparrow back to health, learning that some wild things choose to stay even when the cage door opens. "It doesn't always choose the easy path. Sometimes it chooses the fertile one, even if the soil is rocky. Even if the planting is hard. Because it knows... somehow it knows what will grow there."

Ruth looked at her daughter then, really looked at her
—seeing not just a dutiful girl who tended herbs and cared
for her ailing mother, but a woman with a quiet,
determined fire of her own being kindled behind those
gray eyes. A woman who knew her own mind and was
brave enough to follow her own heart, even into difficult
territory.

She sighed, a soft sound lost in the rattle of the buggy
wheels over frozen ground. "Just be careful, *mei kind*. A
heart that chooses a rocky field must be strong indeed.
Strong enough for drought and storm, as well as sun.
Strong enough for lonely times and hard seasons. Strong
enough to carry not just your own load, but to share his."

"I know, *Mamm*," Susannah whispered. "I know what
I'm choosing."

As they turned down their lane, the buggy lamps
casting shaky circles of light on the frost-silvered ground,
Susannah looked back toward the King farm, now hidden
by a rise of land and the gathering dusk, swallowed by the
night. The taste of fresh cider was still sweet on her
tongue, a memory of community and abundance.

And in her palm, the apple felt like a first, fragile token
of a different kind of harvest yet to come. The thread, so
tentatively offered at the broken plow, had been woven
stronger today, thrumming with potential and promise.
And she had no desire, none at all, to let it go.

The long, patient work of building something real had
begun. Not with grand declarations or easy promises, but
with apples and fences and steady blue eyes that saw her—
truly saw her—and asked her to walk a rocky path
together.

And she would. Gott willing, she would.

CHAPTER 3
The West Pasture

The week between the cider pressing and the promised fence-mending stretched for Susannah like taffy pulled between two hands—each day measured in slow breaths and the silent, steady rhythm of her own churning thoughts. Time had never felt so elastic, so simultaneously endless and fleeting. The perfect Russet apple sat on her windowsill, catching the morning light, a silent, sun-warmed companion to her prayers. It was a tangible thing, a farmer's poetry that spoke more eloquently of care and attention than any flowery love letter from the *Englisch* world ever could.

She found herself touching its smooth skin each morning before dawn prayers, a secret ritual that grounded her in the reality of what was slowly, carefully unfolding between them. The apple had begun to wrinkle slightly, its skin developing the soft creases of age, but she couldn't bring herself to eat it or discard it. It had become a talisman, a physical anchor to that moment by the cider press when he had handed it to her with words meant for her alone: *for the one who calms troubled creatures.*

Was she a troubled creature herself? Perhaps. Her heart certainly felt troubled—restless in a way it had never been before, beating an unfamiliar rhythm that quickened whenever her thoughts turned to a certain tall, quiet farmer and his blue eyes that saw too much.

Ruth's cough deepened with the encroaching chill, settling into her chest with a tenacious, worrying rattle that seemed to sync with the wind in the eaves, becoming part of the house's very song. The sound followed Susannah through her days like a shadow—present at the breakfast table, echoing from the front room while she worked in the kitchen, punctuating the nighttime silence with harsh, tearing sounds that jerked her from sleep.

Susannah spent hours in her still-room, the small attached shed where she dried herbs and mixed remedies, its air perpetually fragrant with memory and hope. The space was her sanctuary, lined with wooden shelves holding mason jars of dried flowers, roots, and leaves—each one labeled in her careful hand, each one a small promise of healing. She prepared a new tincture of elecampane and wild cherry bark, the process a meditation that calmed her restless thoughts.

Each slice of gnarled root, each careful measurement of sharp-scented alcohol drawn from the medicinal supply her grandmother had left her, was an act of devotion—for her mother, certainly, but also, somehow, though she couldn't explain it even to herself, for the quiet, burdened man whose land bordered theirs. She imagined, in her fanciful moments between the practical work, the roots of his apple trees and the roots of her healing herbs reaching toward each other in the dark, unseen soil, drawing from the same hidden waters, connected beneath the surface where no eye could see.

Susannah, steeped as she was in the traditional ways was not against *Englisch* medicine, and recognizing her own limits, had beseeched her *mamm* to talk to Dr Mathews. Her mother would have none of it.

On Tuesday, Esther Coblentz stopped by with the promised jar of apple butter—thick and dark and spiced with cinnamon—and a basket of darning that needed finer eyes than her own aging ones could manage. As they sat in the front room, Ruth dozing in her chair by the stove wrapped in quilts, the older woman's steel needles clicked a steady, probing counterpoint to her words, each click like a small punctuation mark in an unspoken interrogation.

"The cider pressing was a fine gathering," Esther began, not looking up from the sock stretched over her darning egg, her fingers moving with the practiced efficiency of six decades of mending. "A blessing to see the community together, especially with winter at the door. Nathan King seemed... less burdened than usual. He spoke a full sentence to me about the weather—said he was grateful for the dry spell to get the last of the plowing done. It is *gut* for a man alone to have neighbors."

She paused, letting the word 'neighbors' hang in the air like smoke, weighted with implication. Her sharp eyes flicked up briefly to catch Susannah's reaction.

"*Jah*," Susannah agreed neutrally, her own hands busy sorting dried yarrow heads from their stems at the table, the tiny white flowers like miniature suns between her fingers. The delicate work required focus, gave her an excuse not to meet Esther's probing gaze. "The community is its own medicine. We all need each other, especially as the cold comes."

"Barney Stoltzfus was asking after you again at the General Store yesterday." Esther's gaze flicked up sharper now, assessing as a sparrow's. "He is a man ready to build a family. His farm is prosperous, his temperament even— never a cross word, they say. His mother tells me his pantry is already stocked for two winters. A woman could do far worse than a life of steady comfort and cheerful company."

She leaned forward slightly, her voice dropping to something more intimate, more personal. "He would be a shield against hardship, Susannah. There is virtue in a calm harbor, especially for a woman with... with responsibilities." Her eyes cut briefly to Ruth's sleeping form, the unspoken meaning clear: *a woman with a sick mother needs security*.

The words hung in the air, a detailed blueprint for a

safe, predictable future. Susannah thought of Barney's comfortable smile, his easy conversations about crop rotation and the price of feed, the way he laughed readily at any jest. She thought of his well-ordered farm, his cheerful family, the ease that seemed to surround him like an aura. It was appealing in a way, she couldn't deny that.

But then she thought of Nathan's dirt-smeared cheek as he knelt in the mud beside the frightened horse, his intense, wordless focus on a creature in distress, the unspoken understanding that had passed between them like a shared breath. She thought of the way he'd said *you have a way*, with such profound respect, seeing not just what she did but *who she was*. One path was a well-trodden, smooth lane through comfortable terrain. The other was an overgrown track through a rocky field, but it called to her spirit with a resonance she could not deny, a frequency that matched something deep in her own soul.

The Amish talked about listening to the still small voice of Gott and if this inner sense of homecoming wasn't the truest voice she had ever heard, she did not know what was.

"Comfort is a blessing," Susannah said carefully, choosing her words like stepping stones across a swift current. "But faithfulness... it comes in many forms, does it not? Faithfulness to one's own heart, to the gifts Gott gives, even if they lead to harder work. To follow the Almighty's voice wherever that says to go. Even if this leads to a path that others might not understand."

Esther's needles stilled. She studied Susannah for a long moment, her face a map of kindly wrinkles and deep-seated wisdom, seeing perhaps more than Susannah intended to reveal. Then she gave a slow, almost imperceptible nod, a slight dip of her grey head.

"So it does. Your *grossmammi* would say the same. She followed her own path, that one, learning her healing arts when others thought it strange for a young woman to spend so much time with old women and their remedies." Esther's expression softened with memory.

"I remember you telling me when I was a girl that the heart has its own geography. It doesn't always choose the easy path. Sometimes it chooses the fertile one, even if the soil is rocky. Even if the planting is hard. Because it knows somehow what will grow there."

Esther's eyes widened as if to ask: *you remember that? From all that time ago?* Then she nodded again."*Ja.* Just remember, m*ei kind,* faithfulness to a dream can be a lonely path if the dream is not shared. Make certain, when you choose your rocky field, that there's a strong back willing to help you turn that soil. Otherwise, you may find yourself with a field too hard for one pair of hands, no matter how willing."

It was a warning, but not an unkind one. It was the voice of experience, knowing the weight of solitude, the cost of choosing a difficult path and walking it alone.

* * *

The day for the fence-mending dawned not with frost, but with a grey, blustery sky that seemed to press down on the earth like a heavy lid, the wind stripping the last of the tenacious leaves from the oak trees in a rustling, golden rain that carpeted the frozen ground. Susannah woke before dawn, her stomach fluttering with an anticipation she couldn't quite name—part nervousness, part excitement, wholly unfamiliar.

She dressed in her oldest, warmest dove-gray dress, the fabric soft and thin from countless washings, and wrapped a heavy black shawl around her shoulders, pinning it securely against the wind she could already hear howling around the eaves. She packed a small basket with two meat pies wrapped in cloth to keep them warm, a jar of her mother's spiced pear preserves—sweet and sharp and perfect for cold days—and a stoneware bottle of hot sassafras tea, its spicy, root-beer scent promising warmth and comfort.

"You'll catch your death, working in this wind," Ruth fretted from her chair by the stove, her knitting lying forgotten in her lap, her thin hands restless. "It's no day for being out in the open. Feel that wind—it cuts right through to the bone."

"The work will keep me warm," Susannah reassured her, bending to press a kiss to her mother's pale, cool forehead, which felt papery and fragile under her lips. "And the fence won't mend itself. A broken fence means lost sheep come spring. I won't be late."

"It's not the fence I'm worried about," Ruth said quietly, catching her daughter's hand and holding it for a moment, her grip surprisingly strong. Her pale eyes searched Susannah's face. "Be careful, *mei liewe*. Not of the work. Of... of expectations. Of dreams that grow too fast before the ground is ready."

Susannah squeezed her mother's hand gently. "I know, *Mamm*. I'll be careful."

But as she walked out into the biting wind, her basket over her arm, her heart sang a different tune—one that had nothing to do with caution and everything to do with the pull she felt toward the west pasture, toward the man who would be waiting for her there.

***

The walk to the west pasture was longer and lonelier than she'd remembered, following the serpentine property line where the orderly King land met the wilder, wooded edge of the district. The wind bit at her cheeks with teeth like ice and tugged insistently at her *kapp*, threatening to tear it from her head, whispering through the bare branches like gossips sharing secrets. The world felt vast and empty, the sky pressing down, making her feel small and exposed.

She found Nathan already there, his wagon parked on the lane, a pile of new, pale locust posts and a bucket of tools beside him like offerings laid out for some ancient ritual. The locust wood gleamed almost white against the grey day, strong and rot-resistant, the best choice for posts that would need to last decades.

He was wrestling an old, rotted post from the stony ground, his back muscles straining against the thick wool of his coat, the fabric pulling tight across his shoulders with each heave. He hadn't heard her approach over the wind's moan. For a moment, suspended in time, she watched him—the sheer, graceful physicality of his labor, the way his body moved with the practiced efficiency of a lifetime of such work, the solitary figure bent against the vast, grey sky as if in prayer or protest, a lone man against the elements.

Her heart clenched with a fierce, protective tenderness that startled her with its strength, stealing her breath. She wanted, with an intensity that frightened her, to ease his burden. To stand beside him. To share the weight. Even while well knowing someone like blacksmith John Hostetler, whose heart was as big as his muscular shoulders, would be a much more suitable work companion than she. John would also never deny anyone in need. But this was not really about work.

She cleared her throat, the sound small against the elements, nearly lost. Nathan turned, and the look that crossed his face—first surprise, then a swift, bright warmth that momentarily banished the stern, weary lines around his mouth and eyes—made her breath catch in the cold air, made her forget the bite of the wind entirely.

"You came," he said, the words not a question but a statement of wonder, as if he hadn't truly, deep down, believed she would brave the weather and the potential talk for this hard, thankless task. As if he'd expected to spend the day alone after all, despite the promise.

"I said I would," she replied simply, setting her basket down on a flat, grey rock, the stone cold even through the cloth. "The wind is sharper than I reckoned. I brought tea. And food, if you're hungry."

He wiped his earth-stained hands on his trousers and accepted the warm stoneware bottle she offered, their fingers brushing in the exchange. Even through the wool of her mitten, she felt the connection, a current of shared purpose that ran deeper than touch. He took a long drink, his throat working, his eyes closing briefly in simple appreciation that transformed his face, made him look younger, less burdened.

"*Denki*. It's gut. Smells like the woods, those ones at the foot of Hope Valley, in autumn." He opened his eyes and looked at her, really looked at her, seeing the cold already reddening her cheeks, the determination in the set of her chin. "You're sure about this? It's bitter work in this wind. I'd understand if you—"

"I'm sure," she interrupted gently but firmly. "Let's begin. Daylight's wasting."

A slow smile, small but genuine, touched his lips. He nodded and handed back the bottle.

* * *

They worked then, not in the awkward silence of strangers, but in a companionable quiet that was far more intimate and comfortable than the forced chatter of a singing or social gathering. It was the silence of two people who understood that words weren't always necessary, that shared purpose spoke its own language.

He attacked the rocky ground with a digging bar, the *chunk-chunk* of iron striking stone a steady, primitive percussion against the wind's melody, each strike sending small shocks up his arms. Susannah followed behind, steadying the fresh, sweet-smelling locust posts as he set them in the holes, holding them plumb with all her strength—which was considerable, built from years of farm work and lifting her mother—while he packed the stubborn, rocky soil and gravel around their bases with the blunt end of the bar.

It was hard, cold, humbling work that made mockery of vanity. The wind stole her warmth with greedy hands, and her hands grew numb inside her gloves, her fingers becoming clumsy and stiff. A strand of hair, the color of honey, escaped her *kapp* and whipped across her wind-chapped face repeatedly, stinging. Her feet ached from the cold seeping up through the frozen ground. She felt utterly real, stripped of pretense, reduced to the essential self—muscle and will and the stubborn determination not to yield to discomfort. She was a part of the raw landscape, no different from the stones and the struggling grass.

And it felt, strangely, wonderfully, like the truest version of herself she'd ever been.

At one point, as she braced a particularly stubborn post against a gust that seemed determined to topple it, her foot slipped on the loose stones that littered the ground like frozen tears. A gasp was torn from her lips as she felt herself falling. Nathan's hand shot out with surprising speed, grasping her elbow firmly, his grip strong and sure as an oak root, holding her steady until she regained her balance on the treacherous ground.

She looked up, his face close to hers in the grey light, close enough to see the individual whiskers of his beard, the small scar on his chin, the genuine concern etched in the faint lines at the corners of his eyes.

"You're sure you're alright?" he asked, his voice low, nearly lost in the wind's howl, but carrying an intensity that had nothing to do with volume.

"*Jah,*" she breathed, unable to look away from the vivid blue of his gaze so near, feeling as though she might fall again just from the dizziness of his proximity. "Just clumsy."

He didn't let go immediately. His thumb moved, a tiny, unconscious stroke against the rough wool of her sleeve, a gesture of reassurance that sent a shiver through her that had nothing to do with the cold—a warmth that spread from that point of contact through her entire body.

"Not clumsy," he corrected, his voice firm, almost fierce. "The ground is treacherous here. Deceptive. It fools everyone, even those who've walked it all their lives." He finally released her, his hand lingering for a half-

second in the air between them before he turned back to his digging, but she could feel the ghost of his touch, the place where he'd held her humming with a lasting warmth.

* * *

By mid-afternoon, they had set a dozen posts in a defiant line against the weather, each one standing straight and true, a small victory against chaos. The wind had sapped their energy, drying their throats and leaching heat from their bones with relentless efficiency. Susannah's hands ached, her back protested, and her feet had lost most feeling.

They took refuge in the lee of the wagon to eat, sitting close together on a spread-out feed sack, their shoulders nearly touching, the wagon's bulk providing a blessed break from the wind's assault. Susannah handed him a meat pie, its crust still faintly warm from the wrappings. The first bite seemed to revive him, bringing color back to his wind-chapped face.

They ate in a tired, peaceful silence for a few minutes, watching the gunmetal clouds race and churn across the leaden sky like herds of wild horses, sharing the stoneware bottle of tea back and forth, their lips touching the same rim—an intimacy that would have been shocking in another context but here felt natural, necessary.

"Your mother," Nathan said suddenly, not looking at her but at the distant, skeletal outline of the woods, his voice rough from cold and disuse. "Her cough... does it improve with this weather? Or does the cold make it worse?"

The question surprised her with its specificity, its quiet caring. It was not polite small talk. It was genuine concern, the kind that came from personal experience with suffering.

"Some days are better than others. The cold air seizes her chest, makes it harder to draw a full breath. The winter..." She admitted it aloud, the fear she usually kept bundled tight inside. "The winter worries me. Each one is harder than the last."

"My mother had a weak chest," he said, his gaze distant, turned inward to memory. "Asthma, the *Englisch* doctor called it when we finally got her to one."

"Mann refuses to go to the docktor. I try…." Susannah shook her head. "Even Sarah Mathews who blends the old ways and new has come and *Mamm* will have none of it."

"Just like my *mamm*," Nathan nodded. "By the time she would accept help, it was too late… The cold months were always hard—she would struggle for every breath, like drowning on dry land."

He paused, his voice softening with the pain of old

wounds. "I remember my father banking the fires so high the stove glowed red, the metal ticking with heat, making sure her shawls were always warming on the chairback, ready to wrap around her. He'd heat bricks on the stove and wrap them in flannel for her feet, change them every hour through the night. He'd read the almanac to her in the evenings, just to fill the silence with something besides her struggling breath, to give her something to focus on besides the fight for air."

His voice grew quieter still. "It is a heavy thing, to watch someone you love fade and be unable to stop it. To know all your strength means nothing against sickness. A different kind of hard work. The kind that breaks you in places that don't heal."

Tears pricked unexpectedly at the corners of Susannah's eyes, blown cold by the wind before they could fall. He understood. He knew the particular, lonely weight she carried, the weight of the caregiver who must always appear strong while falling apart inside, who watches death approach by inches and can only make the journey more comfortable, not stop it.

"It is," she whispered, the words carried away by the wind almost before they left her lips. "The helplessness is sometimes worse than the work."

"You care for her well," he said, looking at her now, his blue eyes earnest in their scrutiny, seeing her clearly. "Everyone sees it. Your knowledge... it's a gift. Not just for her, but for the whole community." He gestured vaguely back toward his farmyard, encompassing the whole district.

"For the horse the other day—you saw the fear, addressed the fear, not just the symptom. For Jacob Yoder's cow last spring—Noah Albrecht told me it was you who suggested the mullein poultice that cleared the infection when all else failed, when Jacob was ready to put her down. He said you knew just where the mullein grew, in the damp spot by the creek, and that you insisted on gathering it yourself at dawn when the dew was still on it, said that mattered. That kind of knowledge... that's rare."

She flushed, a mixture of pleasure and embarrassment at being seen so clearly, at having her work acknowledged. "It's just old wisdom. *Grossmammi's* notes and her teaching. Nothing special."

"It *is* special," he insisted with a quiet force that brooked no argument, his voice firm. "It's a kind of strength. A quiet strength that mends and waits and knows. That sees the whole picture, not just the broken part."

He looked down at his own work-roughened hands, knuckles scarred from decades of labor, nails edged with soil that never quite washed away. "I have strength for lifting and plowing. For breaking ground and driving posts. But that kind... the kind that sees the sickness in the soil before the crop fails, or reads pain in a breath, or knows which plant will heal which wound... that's a rarer thing. That's wisdom, not just strength." He shook his head, as if the words were failing him, inadequate to capture his meaning.

"It's just a different kind of work," she offered softly, understanding him perfectly, hearing what he couldn't quite articulate. "A necessary kind. We all have our gifts."

"*Jah*," he agreed, relief in his voice at being understood. "A necessary kind."

He fell silent again, but it was a thoughtful, full silence, charged with unspoken things. Finally, he gestured toward the bleak field beyond their new fence line, the expanse of grey-brown earth studded with rocks like broken teeth. "This pasture... it's poor, rocky soil. My father always struggled with it. Called it his 'cross to bear,' said God was testing him with it."

Nathan scooped up a handful of the thin, stony earth, letting it trickle through his fingers like water, watching it fall. "He'd graze it hard every summer, push it to produce, then watch it fail by autumn—the grass thin and weak, barely enough to sustain a small flock. He'd curse it, plow it under, replant, and the cycle would start again."

"But I've been reading," Nathan continued, his voice growing animated in a way she'd never heard before, touched with something that sounded almost like hope. "Talking with Dr David Mathews about the *Englisch* agricultural methods. There are ways. Not our fathers' ways, maybe, but faithful ways. Biblical ways, even— letting the land rest, feeding it what it needs. A sabbatical. The seven year cycle."

He gestured to the field with his free hand, and she could see he was no longer looking at what *was* but what *could be*. "Clover to fix the nitrogen back into the ground— David explained how it works, how the roots actually pull it from the air and feed the soil. Maybe a few dwarf fruit trees on the southern slope for a windbreak and a bonus harvest—apples or pears that could be sold or preserved. It could be better. It could *feed* more than just a few scrawny sheep. It could be... abundant."

He spoke with a passion she hadn't heard before, a vision for the land that went beyond mere maintenance or duty. This was his heart speaking—not just about farming, but about stewardship, about redemption, about taking something worn and tired and hurt and making it fruitful and resilient again. About transformation. His eyes, when he looked at the poor field, saw not what it was, but what, with patience and care and vision, it could become. What it *would* become, if he had his way.

"It sounds like a *gut* plan," she said, captivated by the light of creation in his eyes, by this glimpse of the dreamer hidden beneath the stoic farmer. "A faithful plan that honours the Lord. Working with Gott's design, not against it."

"It will take years," he admitted, the practical farmer returning, but the dreamer still lingered in his tone, coloring it with warmth. "Slow work. Patient work. And help—it's not one-man… one-person work, not if it's to be done right and not just... endured. Not if it's to be done with joy instead of grim determination."

The unspoken question hung between them, as palpable as the solid locust posts they'd just planted, as real as the cold wind that whipped around them. *Will you be part of those years? Will you share this long, patient work? Will you help me dream this dream and make it real?*

Before she could find a response, before she could shape the overwhelming feelings in her chest into words, the sound of buggy wheels grinding on gravel and a cheerful, familiar whistle cut through the wind's monotone like a knife.

Barney Stoltzfus appeared around the bend in the farm lane, his own buggy laden with sacks of seed oats, moving at a brisk pace. He pulled up short when he saw them, his smile wide and easy but his eyes taking in everything—the two of them sitting close together in the shelter of the wagon, the shared basket between them, the intimate landscape of their shared labor.

"Nathan! Susannah! Hard at work, I see." His gaze was friendly, but it missed nothing. "A cold day for fence-mending. Bitter, really. Seems like the wind's blowing straight from the North Pole." He gestured to his load. "I'm just delivering that seed oats we talked about at the pressing, Nathan. I'll put it in your barn for you—no need to stop your work."

His eyes lingered on Susannah, taking in her wind-tangled hair, the dirt on her skirt, the color in her cheeks. "You're looking well, Susannah, though chilled to the bone, I'd wager. This is man's work on a day like this—hard labor in rough conditions. You should be inside by a warm fire with a cup of tea, not out freezing your fingers holding fence posts."

His tone was teasing, even affectionate, but it carried a subtle edge, a reminder of prescribed roles and the comfort of the hearth, of the easier path he represented. The implication was clear: *I would never ask this of you. With me, you'd be protected, sheltered, kept safe from harsh wind and hard labor.*

"All work is Gott's work," she replied evenly, standing and brushing the dirt from her skirt with numb hands, meeting his gaze squarely and refusing to be diminished. "Gott has given me health and strength. And this fence needed doing. The sheep will wander without it come spring. Work doesn't stop because the weather turns."

"That it did," Barney agreed, his smile unwavering, but his gaze was sharp, moving between her wind-tangled hair, her dirt-stained dress, and Nathan's guarded expression. The easy camaraderie of the cider pressing was gone, replaced by a new, unspoken tension that crackled in the cold air like static before a storm.

"Well, I'll be on my way. Don't linger too long in this cold, Susannah. Your mother will worry, and rightly so. This wind cuts to the bone." With a final, inclusive nod that somehow excluded Nathan, he clicked to his horse and moved on down the lane, the cheerful whistle resuming, fainter now, eventually swallowed by the wind.

*　*　*

The spell was broken. The fragile, beautiful intimacy of the afternoon shattered by the arrival of a rival who held all the cards of convention, ease, and community approval. The wind suddenly felt ten degrees colder, finding every gap in Susannah's clothing.

Nathan watched the buggy disappear around the bend, his jaw tight, a muscle working in his cheek, his hands clenched at his sides. He turned back to her, his expression grim, the shutters coming down over his eyes like storm shutters battened against a gale.

"He's right. You should go in. The wind is getting worse, and you're not dressed for much more of this. I can finish the rest myself." His voice was gentle, but final. He was retreating, pulling back behind the high walls of his solitary responsibility, perhaps fearing the gossip Barney's sighting would spark, perhaps to protect her from it.

Disappointment, sharp and cold as the stones underfoot, stabbed through her chest. She had offered her help, her companionship, her partnership, and it was being handed back to her, wrapped in practical concern and masculine pride.

She simply nodded, her throat tight with unshed words, and began gathering the basket, the leftover pie suddenly seeming foolish, childish.

He helped her, his touch now formal, careful, scrupulously avoiding contact. As she turned to leave, the weight of the unsaid words crushing her, making it hard to breathe, he spoke again, his voice barely audible over the moaning wind, as if the words were ripped from him against his will.

"The plan for the pasture... it's a good one. I've drawn sketches. Rough ones, but they show the layout—where the clover would go, where the trees would stand, how the water would flow." He paused, the silence stretching. "I'd... I'd value your thoughts. You see things others miss. The land, the plants... you see the life in them, the connections. The web some of the older women talk about."

It was an offering, a thread thrown across the growing, windy distance between them. A lifeline. She met his eyes and saw the conflict there—the sincere desire for her connection warring with the fear of complication, of drawing her into his difficult world, of causing trouble for her in the eyes of people like Barney and Veronica, of exposing her to hardship.

She held his gaze, refusing to let him look away, refusing to let him retreat completely. "I would like to hear more about it," she said firmly, her voice clear despite the wind. "And see the sketches. Very much. Another time."

A flicker of profound relief, quickly masked, in his eyes. "*Jah*," he said, the word a pledge, a promise. "Another time. Soon."

* * *

The walk home was long and lonely, the wind now feeling personal and hostile, pushing against her as if trying to drive her back, to make her turn around. The warmth of the afternoon, the shared vision of clover and fruit trees, felt like a dream dreamed by someone else— beautiful but insubstantial, already fading.

Reality was the disapproving glance she imagined from Veronica Zook when word reached her which then in turn would be passed around Miracle Creek quicker than a cold. Reality was the persistent, rattling cough of her mother waiting at home, a sound that would greet her before she even opened the door. Reality was the easy, suitable future offered by Barney Stoltzfus's steady smile and well-stocked pantry, and the solitary, difficult, rocky path leading to Nathan King's west pasture and an uncertain dream.

Yet, as she clutched her shawl tight against the gale, leaning into the wind's fury, the memory of his hand on her elbow, the light in his eyes when he spoke of the land's potential, bloomed within her like a hardy, wintergreen plant that refused to yield to frost. She knew, with a certainty that settled deep in her bones, that her choice was already made.

Her heart, foolishly and faithfully, had already taken root in that stony ground. The real work—the long, patient tending of something fragile and precious against the wind of opinion and circumstance—had only just begun. And she would not, could not, turn back now.

The rocky field called to her. And she would answer.

CHAPTER 4
A Sprained Ankle and a Shared Secret

The week following the fence-mending was a tapestry of dull anxiety for Susannah, woven with threads of hope and fear in equal measure, the pattern shifting with each passing day. The memory of Nathan's swift retreat into formality haunted her—the way his expression had shuttered when Barney appeared, the careful distance he'd put between them afterward.

The specter of Barney Stoltzfus's pointed observation seemed to hang over everything, a cloud that wouldn't dissipate. And underneath it all, constant as her own heartbeat, was the worsening, rattling cage of her mother's chest, each cough a reminder of fragility and time running out, and each refusal to see Dr David Mathews a new knife twisting in her chest.

These elements wove together into a heavy cloak she couldn't shake, even in the warmth of the kitchen, even during her prayers. She found herself standing at windows, staring toward the direction of the King farm, wondering if Nathan was thinking of her, if he regretted their afternoon together, if the sketches he'd mentioned even existed or if that had been a polite fiction to ease their parting.

The community, a living organism as perceptive as any of her sensitive herbs, seemed to buzz with a quiet, speculative energy that made her skin prickle whenever she went to the store or encountered neighbors. At church that Sunday, Esther Coblentz's glances held less motherly concern and more pointed curiosity, her eyes following Susannah with an intensity that felt like a physical touch. Veronica Zook and Dorcas Hershberger stopped talking when she approached, she obviously being the topic of their animated discussion. Emma Albrecht while picking up more mending, asked with wide-eyed innocence if Susannah had gotten the chill that was going around from her time in the west pasture, the question loaded with implication.

Even Bishop Samuel Lapp during his sermon on steadfastness and knowing one's path, gave her a longer, more contemplative look that made her cheeks burn and her hands twist in her lap. She felt exposed, as if the feelings growing in her heart were written on her forehead for all to read.

Nathan was a ghost in the usual places, conspicuous in his absence. His broad shoulders were absent from the back bench at the Sunday service, his usual spot conspicuously empty. His buggy was not among the cluster at the general store when she went for salt and thread, though she found herself looking for it, her heart sinking each time it wasn't there. He wasn't at the barn raising for the Millers' new addition, though his strength would have been a boon and such events were rarely missed. It was as if, having ventured a fleeting glimpse of connection, he had withdrawn completely into the fortress of his farm, fortifying his walls against both the weather and the wagging tongues.

The silence from his direction felt louder than any word, a roaring absence that filled her thoughts. Had she imagined the warmth in his eyes? Had she misread everything? The doubt crept in like frost, chilling her from the inside.

Susannah threw herself into work with almost desperate intensity, the only antidote she knew for restless wondering. She harvested the last of the precious comfrey and valerian roots before the ground froze iron-hard, her fingers numb as she brushed soil from their gnarled, twisted shapes, each one looking like something ancient and wise pulled from the earth's memory. She distilled tinctures until her small still-room smelled like a concentrated forest, pungent and green and alive—basil and thyme, lavender and chamomile, each one carefully labeled and dated in her neat hand.

She tended to her mother with a focused tenderness that bordered on desperation, measuring each breath Ruth took, each spoonful of broth she consumed, watching for any sign of improvement or decline with the intensity of a sentinel. Yet, the quiet hollow in her chest remained, echoing with the memory of a shared meat pie in the lee of a wagon, the sound of a man's voice—husky with rare passion—dreaming of clover and fruit trees, and the feel of rocky soil giving way under a new post, planted together.

* * *

On Friday, a brittle, sunny morning that glittered with false promise—the kind of day where the light was bright but gave no warmth—the answer to her unspoken wondering came not in a buggy or a note, but in the form of young Samuel Andrews, Miracle Creek postman Joseph Andrew's boy. He came panting up to their door on his scooter, his breath pluming in the sharp air like steam from a kettle, his cheeks red from exertion and cold.

"Susannah! *Mamm* says can you come quick? It's Nathan! He's had a mishap with the manure spreader in the back forty. He's hurt his leg something awful, but Dr Mathews and his wife are both over in Hope Valley dealing with a seesaw delivery."

"A seesaw?" It took a moment before understanding dawned. "Ach *jah*, a Caesarean? Bishop Waver's wife in Hope Valley?" Nance Weaver was expecting twins and in her 40s was an older mother so the risks of complications with her pregnancy were far greater. Susannah silently thanked Gott that the bishop was wise enough to let *Englisch* medicine help and asked that Gott would guide the *doktor* and his midwife wife's hands. But her mind was already back on Nathan. *What—?*

The boy shrugged but the boy's eyes were wide with the importance of his mission. "*Mamm* thought of you straight off, with your remedies and your... your way with hurt things."

Susannah's heart seized, a cold fist clenching around it, driving the air from her lungs. *Nathan.* Hurt. The words seemed to echo in her skull, drowning out everything else. Without a word, her healer's instincts overriding panic, she grabbed her heavy cloak from the peg and the worn leather satchel of supplies that always stood ready by the door—her grandmother's bag, really, passed down through generations of healing women, its leather smooth from decades of use.

"Tell your *Mamm* I'm coming," she said, already moving toward the barn where their old pony, Daisy, dozed in her stall. "Go ahead—I'll follow as fast as I can."

She barely remembered hitching up the cart, her hands moving with automatic efficiency while her mind raced ahead. *How badly hurt? What if it's broken? What if—* She cut off that thought savagely. Speculation helped no one. She needed to see him, assess him, *help* him.

* * *

The ride to the King farm felt interminable, each jolt of the cart wheels over frozen ruts echoing the dread in her stomach like a drum. The "back forty" was the farthest, lowest field, a place of rich black soil used for spreading nutrient-dense manure in the fall. It was a mucky, lonely spot, isolated from the main farmyard.

She found the scene there, and her heart clenched at the sight: the large, wheeled manure spreader was tilted at a drunken angle, one massive wheel sunk deep in a hidden, muddy sinkhole disguised by frost—a trap waiting to catch the unwary. Nathan sat on the frozen ground nearby, his back against the spreader's heavy iron frame, his face pale and set in sharp lines of pain and simmering frustration that tightened his jaw. His right leg was stretched out before him, the work boot still on, but the ankle area already showing an ominous, swollen bulge straining against the stiff leather like something trying to escape.

Old man Graber was there too, having come over from his adjacent field when he saw the trouble, his own work abandoned. He was calmly unhitching the confused, snorting team from the stuck equipment, speaking to them in low, soothing tones.

"Susannah," Joseph Andrews said, relief softening his normally stoic features. "*Gut.* You're here. He won't listen to sense. Says it's just a twist, that he'll walk it off. Stubborn as his father ever was."

Nathan's head snapped up at her arrival, his blue eyes clouded with pain but flashing with a complex mixture of emotions—shame at his own helplessness, anger at his weakness, and something else, something that looked achingly like relief, a profound gratitude that he quickly tried to mask behind a grimace.

"It's nothing. A twist," he said, the words automatic, defensive. "I don't need—"

"Let me be the judge of that," Susannah interrupted, her voice assuming the calm, firm tone she used with skittish animals and fretful children—a tone that brooked no argument, that commanded obedience through sheer certainty. She knelt in the frozen mud beside him, the cold seeping instantly through her skirts, numbing her knees, but she didn't care. She opened her medical satchel with a familiar, decisive *click* that seemed loud in the tense quiet.

"Joseph can you get his boot off? Carefully. It might be the only thing holding the swelling in place right now."

With Joseph's strong, steady hands providing counter-pressure at the heel, they managed to work the boot off, Nathan sucking in a sharp hiss of air through clenched teeth, his hands fisting in the dirt beside him. The ankle was badly sprained, already blooming into a spectacular bruise of livid purple and angry red that spread like spilled wine, swollen to nearly twice its normal size, the skin tight and shiny.

Susannah's practiced hands moved over the injury with professional detachment despite the way her heart ached at his pain, her touch clinical but gentle as a whisper. She palpated the bones carefully, feeling him flinch but detecting no grating misalignment, no sickening give that would indicate a break. Not broken, thank God, but a severe, painful ligament injury that would hobble him for weeks if not properly cared for.

"You will not be walking on this for a week, at least," she stated, looking directly into his eyes, holding his gaze with her healer's authority, with the full weight of her knowledge. "And you will need to keep it elevated and iced to bring the swelling down, or it will stiffen and plague you all winter, and into planting time. You could do permanent damage if you're foolish about this."

"I have work—" he began, the protest automatic, born of a lifetime of duty that never paused for weakness or inconvenience.

"The work will wait," old man Graber interrupted, his tone leaving no room for discussion, channeling the voice of every sensible farmer who knew the difference between dedication and foolishness. He went back to the team and walked far ahead guiding them to the barn.

Joseph stood, brushing his hands on his trousers. "A crippled farmer is no use to anyone, Nathan. You know that as well as I do. Susannah is right."

He looked at the stuck spreader, then back at Nathan's pale face. "The ground's freezing solid. That rig won't move till spring thaw anyway. Let it be. The farm will still be here tomorrow, and the day after that."

Nathan looked from Joseph's stern, sensible face, then flicked to Susannah's resolved one, seeing no mercy there, only determination. The fight drained out of him visibly, his shoulders sagging, replaced by a weary, defeated surrender that was somehow more intimate than any vulnerability he'd yet shown. It was the surrender of a man who had carried everything alone for too long and had finally, catastrophically, reached his limit. He gave a single, curt nod, his eyes dropping to his misshapen ankle.

* * *

Between them, Susannah and Joseph helped Nathan to his feet—or rather, his foot. He hopped on his good leg, his immense weight heavy and awkward between them, leaning heavily. His arm slung around the Joseph's shoulders for main support, but his other hand came to rest on Susannah's arm for balance. The contact, even through layers of wool and worry, was electric, charged with all the unspoken feelings that had grown between them. Despite the circumstances, despite the pain he must be feeling, she was acutely aware of his touch, of his closeness, of the way he seemed to lean into her just slightly more than strictly necessary.

They half-carried, half-hopped him to her cart and got him settled awkwardly in the back, his injured leg propped on a sack of feed that Joseph retrieved from his own wagon, cushioned as much as possible.

"I and old man Graber will see to your team and get this mess sorted later," Joseph said to Nathan, his voice dropping to a more personal timbre, man to man. "You listen to her now. Don't be a fool about this."

He then turned to Susannah, giving her a meaningful, almost paternal look that spoke volumes. "His *daadi haus* is empty. Clean. It's closer to the main house than his own quarters. It would be... easier. More proper."

It was a practical suggestion that also offered a crucial sliver of propriety. Treating him in the empty grandparents' cottage, with its separate door and its proximity to his Aunt Edna in the main house, was a world apart from being alone with him in his own bachelor quarters. Susannah nodded her thanks, understanding the unspoken protection in the offer, the way Joseph was sheltering both their reputations.

* * *

They got him into the small, cold *daadi haus* with considerable difficulty, Nathan gritting his teeth against the pain, his face grey by the time they maneuvered him inside. The air inside was still and dusty, smelling of old wood and absence, of a space that had been waiting empty for too long.

Susannah built a quick, bright fire in the tiny pot-bellied stove, coaxing the kindling to catch, feeding it carefully until flames leaped and crackled, while Nathan sat stiffly on the edge of the narrow bed, watching her movements with an intensity that made her hyperaware of every gesture, his hat in his hands, turning it slowly.

The silence was thick, charged with his acute pain and the weight of their shared, unspoken history. When the room had warmed from tomb-like to merely chilly, she set to work with the focused efficiency that always claimed her when healing. She pumped cool water into a basin at the small sink, her movements practiced. She cleaned his ankle with a soft cloth, her touch clinical but gentle, noting the heat radiating from the inflamed skin like a small stove.

From her stores, she prepared a poultice with hands that knew the work by heart: the sharp, green smell of crushed comfrey leaves for healing and bone-knitting, the subtle tang of arnica for bruising and pain, mixed with cool, grey clay from the creek bank to draw out the heat and soothe. The familiar scents filled the small room, transforming it from a place of absence into a place of healing.

As she applied the messy, healing plaster, wrapping his ankle snugly with clean linen strips in a careful figure-eight pattern, she spoke softly, her voice a steady anchor in his sea of pain and frustration.

"This needs to stay on for a few hours, at least through the evening. I'll make you a tea for the pain and inflammation—willow bark, mostly, which works much like the *Englisch* aspirin. And a little valerian root to help you rest, because you need to sleep to heal. The body does its best work while we sleep."

"You always know what to do," he murmured, his voice ragged with more than pain, roughened with emotion he was too tired to hide. He watched her hands as if they were performing a miracle, as if she were weaving magic instead of simply applying plants to injury.

"It's what I was taught," she said, not looking up, focusing on the secure but not-too-tight knot she was tying, making sure the bandage would stay but not cut off circulation. "It's just plants and patience. Anyone could learn it."

"It's more than that," he insisted, his voice gaining a little strength, a quiet fierceness entering it. He was quiet for a long moment, the only sound the crackle of the fire and the wind outside. "I've been... keeping to myself. Since the pasture. Since Barney came by."

Her hands stilled in her lap, the leftover linen a white pool against her grey skirt. She finally met his gaze, seeing the conflict there, raw and exposed—the vulnerability of a man unused to explaining himself, unused to admitting weakness of any kind. "I noticed."

"Barney Stoltzfus..." He swallowed hard, looking away toward the small, frost-rimed window, struggling with the words as if they were in a foreign language he barely spoke. "He represents the right path. The easy one. For you. I saw it in his face that day—saw the way he looked at you, at us. He sees a future there, clear as day. A straight, smooth furrow. A comfortable life with laughter and ease."

His jaw worked. "A future I have no right to... to cloud with my rocky ground and my silences and my... my burdens. You deserve better than a man who's already married to his land, who can offer you nothing but hard work and lean years while we try to make something grow where everything has failed before."

He spoke not with self-pity, but with a grim, resigned conviction that he was stating an obvious, difficult truth. His humility, his willingness to step aside for what he perceived as her better, easier good, touched her deeply— and simultaneously sparked a bright, hot flare of frustration in her chest that surprised her with its intensity.

"Do you think so little of my own mind, Nathan King?" she asked, her voice low but sharp, cutting through his resignation like a blade. "That I am a child who cannot read the map of her own life? That I cannot see the path before me—both the smooth lane and the rocky track— and choose, with a clear heart and open eyes, which one to walk? Do you think me so weak, so foolish?"

His eyes flew back to hers, startled, as if she had physically shaken him. "Nee. I think... I think the world would say I am a poor choice," he said, the words blunt, unvarnished. "A man married to his land before any woman, with little laughter and less conversation to offer. A man who spends his days talking to crops and livestock more than people, whose inheritance is as much burden as blessing. Whose house is empty and whose table is quiet."

"And I," she countered, a hint of a wry, understanding smile touching her lips despite the gravity of the moment, "am a woman who spends her days talking to herbs and sick people, who sees visions in the veins of leaves and reads stories in the cough of the wind and the color of the soil. Whose dowry is a satchel of weeds and a head full of old wives' tales that half the community thinks are too close to superstition."

She leaned forward slightly, her grey eyes holding his blue ones captive. "We are neither of us, I think, much for idle chatter or fancy socials or easy, comfortable lives. We see deeper than that. We care about things that can't be measured in bushels or coins."

A ghost of a smile, the first genuine one she'd seen since his injury, touched his own mouth, transforming his stern face, lighting it from within. "*Jah*. That is true. That is... very true."

The tension broke like a spring thaw, replaced by a warmer, more vulnerable understanding. She busied herself preparing the tea over the small stove, the bitter, clean scent of willow bark filling the room, mixing with the woodsmoke and the herbal plaster. The familiar work steadied her.

"You asked for my thoughts on your pasture," she said, shifting the subject to safer, yet profoundly intimate, ground, breaking the silence that had grown too heavy. "About the clover and the fruit trees. Before we were... interrupted by Barney."

He took the offered tin cup, his fingers brushing hers in

the transfer, a touch now conscious and acknowledged, lingering just a heartbeat longer than necessary. "I've been reading the agricultural pamphlets David Mathews gets from the *Englisch* world," he said, sipping the bitter brew without complaint, his face relaxing slightly as the warmth spread through him. "There's a method... they call it companion planting. The *Englisch* have studied it, but it's really just old wisdom—the kind your grandmother would have known. Certain things grow better together. Support each other. Protect each other from pests and disease."

He paused, gathering his thoughts, his eyes growing distant with the vision. "Like beans on cornstalks—the beans give nitrogen back to the soil that the corn depletes; the corn gives the beans a sturdy pole to climb toward the sun. One gives sustenance, the other gives structure. Neither could do as well alone. Together, they thrive."

Susannah sat in the room's only chair, a simple ladder-back with a woven rush seat, facing him across the small space. She wrapped her hands around her own cup, drawing warmth from it, watching his face as he spoke. "A good partnership," she said softly, the words carrying layers of meaning. "Each giving what the other needs. Not taking, but exchanging. Making the whole stronger than the parts could ever be separately."

He held her gaze over the rim of his cup, his blue eyes intense, searching hers. "*Jah*. Exactly."

He took a deep breath, as if steeling himself for a confession, for laying bare something he'd kept protected. "This farm... it was my father's dream. His life's blood. When he died, it became my duty. My burden." The admission was stark, painful. "For a year, I've just been trying not to fail him. To keep it exactly as he left it, every fence wire tight, every field in its rotation, every tool in its place. Like a... a shrine to his memory."

He looked down at his swollen, wrapped ankle, a

tangible symbol of struggle and imperfection and the cost of carrying everything alone. "But the broken plow... the rocky pasture... this." He gestured to his injury. "They're not his problems anymore. They're mine. And the ideas for fixing them... the clover, the trees, the companion planting... they're mine, too, not his."

His voice grew stronger. "For the first time, I'm not just keeping his dream alive like a museum piece, like something under glass that can't be touched or changed. I'm... I'm starting to dream my own. For this land. For what it could become, not just what it was."

The confession was monumental. In his culture, where tradition was sacred and a father's ways were scripture, where change came slowly and only with the community's blessing, this was a quiet, profound revolution. It was him emerging from his father's long, demanding shadow, not in rebellion, but in faithful succession, becoming his own man while honoring what came before.

"I think that is a *gut* thing, Nathan," Susannah said softly, her heart swelling with admiration and something deeper, something that felt like the beginning of love taking root. "A living thing must grow, or it dies. Even a dream. *Especially* a dream. A dream that doesn't grow becomes a prison."

He looked at her then, his eyes clear and fiercely intent, burning with something that made her breath catch. "A dream needs a reason beyond just survival. It needs... a purpose. A hope for a harvest you can't yet see, for fruit you won't taste for years, for shade tree you won't sit under for twenty summers." He leaned forward slightly, the bed frame creaking, closing the distance between them. "It needs a shared reason. A shared vision. It needs... partnership."

The air between them vibrated with the unsaid, with meanings that had nothing to do with agriculture and everything to do with the future, with lives intertwined, with promises not yet spoken but already felt. He was no longer talking just about clover or apple trees. He was talking about a life. About *their* life.

"Hope," she whispered, holding his gaze, feeling as though she were standing on the edge of something vast and terrifying and utterly right, "is a stubborn plant, Nathan. It can grow in rocky soil. It just needs a little more care, a little more patience. And someone to tend it faithfully."

For a long, suspended moment, they simply looked at each other, the crackle of the fire the only sound in the tiny room. The wall between them was down, completely demolished. The shared secret of his vision for the land— and the unspoken question of her place within that vision —was now alive in the space between them, acknowledged, breathed in, made real.

Finally, he broke the gaze, a faint, uncharacteristic blush tingeing his cheekbones, making him look younger, less burdened. "You should go. Your mother will need you... and the talk..." He trailed off, his concern for her reputation clear in his troubled eyes.

She nodded, standing. But before she left, she took from her satchel a small, linen-wrapped packet tied with string. "This is more willow bark tea. Steep it strong, twice a day." She placed it on the small table by the bed. Then, from a smaller pouch, she produced another packet, this one softer, fragrant.

"And this," she said, placing it gently beside the first, her fingers lingering on it, "is a salve for the bruising, once the hot swelling goes down in a day or two. I made it with lamb's ear and lavender from my garden." *My garden.* It was a piece of herself, of her own nurtured plot of earth, she was giving him. A piece of her world, offered freely.

He looked at the humble packets as if they were rare

jewels, more valuable than any store-bought medicine or *Englisch* doctor's prescription. His hand reached out, not quite touching them, hovering. "*Denki*, Susannah," he said, his voice thick with emotion he didn't try to hide. "For... for everything. For coming. For not listening to me when I said it was nothing. For... for seeing past my foolish pride."

At the door, she turned, her hand on the cold latch, looking back at him sitting on that narrow bed, his injured leg propped up, his eyes on her. "I'll come by tomorrow to change the poultice. And to check on my patient." She allowed a small, firm, no-nonsense smile to surface. "Do not argue. Do not try to get up and work. I will know if you do, and I will be very displeased."

He didn't argue. He simply nodded, his eyes holding hers across the small room, a world of promise and newfound courage shining in their blue depths. "I will be here," he said, and it was a vow, a commitment to let himself be cared for, to accept help, to not face everything alone anymore.

* * *

The ride home through the gathering twilight was filled with a quiet, soaring joy that even the persistent, worried thought of her mother's cough could not diminish. The sky was painted in shades of rose and lavender, the kind of sunset that seemed to promise better days ahead.

Nathan King did not offer easy words or a smooth, paved path into an uncomplicated future. He offered shared purpose. A partnership where each brought their unique strength to the other's weakness—her healing knowledge for his physical hurts and his isolation, his dream of abundance for her quiet faithfulness and her need for meaning. He saw her, not just as a woman to be courted, but as a potential partner in the sacred, gritty dream of a fruitful land and a purposeful life.

It was not a proposal, not yet. It was something more foundational. A covenant of understanding, sown in rocky soil and watered with honesty and pain and the slow revelation of hidden hearts.

As she guided Daisy home through the deepening dusk, the last of the sunset breaking through the clouds in a final, glorious fanfare of orange and gold, painting the frozen fields in transient, fiery beauty, Susannah's hand curled around the memory of his touch, of his trust.

The rocky west pasture, she thought, her heart full to bursting, might just be the most fertile ground for hope after all. The sprained ankle was a painful setback, but it had broken open something far more important: the sealed chamber of Nathan King's lonely heart, letting the light—and Susannah Mast—finally, fully, stream in.

And she would return tomorrow, and the day after that, to tend not just his injury, but the fragile, growing thing between them. To water the seeds of a shared dream with patience and care, until they took root too deep to ever be torn out.

CHAPTER 5
The Thanksgiving Service

Nathan's sprained ankle became a silent, shared pivot around which their worlds slowly, irrevocably turned, like the earth tilting toward spring. True to her word, Susannah visited the King farm each afternoon under the practical, unassailable guise of medical care—a purpose so obviously necessary that even the most suspicious gossip could find no fault with it. Even though Veronica Zook could find fault with near everything. The first few visits were conducted with a careful, choreographed formality that felt almost theatrical, Ruth accompanying her in the buggy for propriety's sake, her presence a protective shield against wagging tongues.

Ruth would sit in the main house's neat, spare kitchen with a cup of tea and a piece of whatever simple cake Nathan's Aunt Edna had baked, talking in low tones with the elderly woman who kept house for him with brisk efficiency. Aunt Edna was a widow herself, quiet and observant, her dark eyes missing nothing but her tongue blessedly restrained. While they talked of weather and community news, Susannah tended to her patient in the *daadi haus*, the separate building providing just enough privacy for healing while maintaining the appearance of propriety.

The arrangement was a latticework of convention, carefully constructed, allowing the delicate vine of their connection to grow unseen behind the protective screen of medical necessity. It was a dance they both understood— the careful steps required to court in a community where every action was observed, every deviation from tradition noted and discussed.

But even with this chaperonage, the moments alone in the small cottage were a stolen haven, precious beyond measure. Nathan was a model patient, if a restless one. He followed her instructions with a farmer's disciplined obedience—elevating his foot on a sack of grain, applying the cold compresses she left wrapped in cloth, drinking the bitter willow bark tea without complaint. But she could see the frustration in the rigid set of his shoulders, in his gaze constantly straying to the window where his dormant fields lay under the grey sky, waiting. His hands, unused to idleness, would fidget with the edge of his quilt or turn his hat brim round and round, restless energy seeking an outlet.

"The livestock are being tended," she reminded him on the third visit, unwrapping the old poultice and examining the ankle with satisfaction. The swelling had gone down considerably, the angry purple fading to a sickly yellow-green. "Joseph Andrews checks on them morning before his rounds. Old man Graber in the evenings. Your Aunt Edna feeds the chickens. The farm hasn't forgotten you exist just because you're sitting still for once in your life."

"It feels that way," he admitted, his voice rough with disuse and frustration. "Like if I'm not there, watching, working, it will all fall apart. Like I'm... failing."

"You're healing," she corrected firmly, applying the new salve—her lavender one now, the swelling sufficiently reduced—with gentle, circular motions that made him draw in a sharp breath. "That's work too. Important work. You can't pour from an empty cup, Nathan. Sometimes the cup needs refilling."

He looked at her then, really looked at her, seeing not just the healer but the woman, the person who seemed to understand the particular tyranny of responsibility, the guilt that came with rest. "You speak from experience."

"I do," she said quietly, wrapping the ankle with fresh

linen. "Caring for *Mamm...* some days I feel if I stop moving, if I let my guard down for even a moment, I'll lose her. That my vigilance is the only thing keeping her breathing. It's not true, I know that in my head. But the heart doesn't always listen to the head."

"No," he agreed softly. "It doesn't."

* * *

Their conversations, once they moved past the clinical details of his care, began to weave a new, stronger understanding, thread by thread, creating something whole from separate strands. He showed her the dog-eared agricultural pamphlets from Dr Mathews, pointing out passages with a work-roughened finger, his voice growing animated in a way she'd never heard in public as he explained the science of crop rotation and soil amendments—the way nitrogen moved through the system, how different plants fed or depleted different minerals, the complex dance of growth and renewal.

She, in turn, shared her rooted, intuitive knowledge—which wild plants like sorrel or plantain indicated poor or rich soil, how the presence of certain fungi could tell a story of moisture and decay, the way peppermint in the livestock's bedding could deter flies and soothe their nerves. She explained how chickweed thrived in disturbed soil, how nettles meant nitrogen-rich earth, how the health of the land could be read like a book if you knew the language.

"See this diagram?" she said one afternoon, her finger tracing a cross-section of a hedgerow in one of his pamphlets, their heads bent close together over the page. "You spoke of fruit trees on the southern slope for a windbreak. But if you planted serviceberries and chokecherries at the outer edge, closer to the woods, they'd feed the birds all summer—robins, waxwings, thrushes.

And the birds," she looked up, her gray eyes alight with the excitement of connection, of seeing the pattern, "they would repay you by eating the caterpillars and beetles from your apple trees before they could do real damage. It's a bargain. A partnership. It's all connected—every piece supports another."

She paused. "Gott… his perfect design is truly amazing. To think that some out in the *Englisch* world cannot see the intelligent hand at work behind it." She shook her head. "Nature is amazing."

He looked from the technical drawing to her face, his expression one of pure wonder, as if she had translated a secret text written in a language he'd been struggling to learn. "You see the whole picture," he murmured, his voice filled with something close to reverence. "Not just the single field, or the lone plant, but the... the web of it. The give and take. The way everything fits together like pieces of a puzzle."

"It's how my grandmother taught me," she said softly, closing the pamphlet but leaving her hand near his on the table, close but not quite touching. "She said Gott didn't make a single thing without a purpose and a place in the circle. Every creature, every plant, every stone has its role. Healing, she said, was just helping things—people, animals, even land—find their right balance again. Restoring them to their place in the pattern."

"Balance," he echoed, his gaze intent on her, seeing the echo of that wise woman in her granddaughter's features, in the tilt of her head, in the way her hands moved when she spoke. "A farm out of balance is a sick farm. The soil gets tired and depleted, the animals get thin and susceptible to disease, the weeds take over because the good plants are too weak to compete."

He paused, his voice dropping to something more personal, more vulnerable. "A life out of balance..." He didn't finish, but the implication hung heavy between them, palpable as the herb-scented air. His life had been all duty, no heart, a straight furrow of obligation plowed year after year through the same exhausted soil. Hers had been all care for others, with a quiet, hollow chamber reserved for her own unseen dreams, her own needs left untended.

* * *

By the end of the week, Nathan could hobble short distances with a stout crutch Joseph Andrews had expertly fashioned from a forked branch of hickory, the wood smooth and strong and perfectly fitted to his height. The vivid, stormy bruising on Nathan's ankle was fading to a greenish-yellow, a topographical map of his mishap that looked worse than it felt. He was healing, the resilience of his body asserting itself.

The Sunday before Thanksgiving, the community would hold its annual Thanksgiving service, a solemn and deeply joyous gathering to express collective gratitude for the harvest's bounty before the deep, introspective quiet of winter set in. It was one of the year's most important services, a time when even the most reclusive members made the effort to attend, when the community gathered as one body to acknowledge their dependence on Providence.

It was also a time when the slowed rhythms of courtship, paused by the urgent work of harvest, often re-awakened with intention, with families looking toward spring and new beginnings, assessing which young people might be suited, which paths might merge.

Susannah felt a nervous flutter like a caged sparrow in her chest as she dressed that morning, her hands trembling slightly as she pinned her *kapp*. Her best deep-blue dress, the color of a twilight sky just after sunset, felt suddenly too fine, too noticeable, the fabric too smooth against her skin. Her freshly pressed *kapp* seemed too stark and white against her blonde hair, too conspicuous. She felt exposed, as if her feelings were visible, as if everyone would look at her and simply *know*.

Ruth, though still pale and moving slowly, her breath sometimes catching in her chest, insisted on attending. "We have much to be thankful for," she said, her eyes on her daughter with a knowing, gentle exhaustion that spoke of a mother's intuition. "Not least a certain stubborn farmer who is walking again, praise Gott. We must give thanks in company, where thanks belong."

* * *

The service was held in the Beilers' large bank barn, cleared of livestock and swept clean until the wooden planks gleamed, the air still carrying the sweet, dusty scent of hay and the earthy smell of animals recently moved— comforting, familiar smells that spoke of home and sustenance. It was chilly despite the press of bodies, but warmed by the collective presence of the congregation— the soft rustle of dresses, the solid presence of men in black coats, the whispered shuffles of children being shushed, the clearing of throats, the creak of benches.

Susannah's eyes, accustomed to scanning a room for signs of discomfort or need, found Nathan immediately. He was seated with the men on the far side of the barn, the traditional division of the sexes, his crutch leaning against the bench beside him like a faithful hound. He looked both handsome and severe in his black Sunday coat, his hair neatly combed back, still damp from his morning washing, catching the light. His posture was straight despite his injury, dignified, present.

His gaze swept the women's section with what appeared

to be casual observation, but she knew better—she could see the restless searching in it, the slight tension in his jaw. When his eyes found hers across the crowded space, a current, silent and powerful as lightning, passed between them. The air seemed to crackle with it. He gave the smallest, almost imperceptible nod, a private acknowledgment that made her breath catch and her palms grow warm inside her gloves, her heart suddenly hammering against her ribs.

Barney Stoltzfus, seated a few rows ahead of Nathan with the other unmarried men, turned slightly just as Nathan's gaze found Susannah. He caught the exchange, the unmistakable connection passing between them across the crowded barn. His pleasant, open face tightened almost imperceptibly, a slight narrowing of the eyes, a thinning of the lips, a hardening of his jaw, before he turned back resolutely to face the ministers on the plain wooden bench at the front.

The message was clear: he had seen, and he understood, and he was not pleased. The easy path was closing, and they all knew it.

* * *

The service was long and moving, filled with the slow, solemn harmonies of German hymns sung from memory —songs of gratitude for seed and sun, for rain and yield, for the faithful cycle of planting and harvest that sustained them. The voices rose and fell in complex harmonies that had been sung for centuries, connecting them to generations past and generations yet to come. The sermons, delivered by the ministers in their traditional, unchanging rotation, recounted the year's specific blessings and trials with the measured cadence of men who knew their flock intimately.

Bishop Miller, the final speaker, come the 3 miles over

- 81 -

from Hope Valley, stood with his hands clasped before him, his weathered face solemn, his voice a deep, weathered instrument that filled the barn. He spoke of the tangible bounty of the land—the full corn cribs that would feed livestock through winter, the fattened livestock that would provide meat and milk, the cellar shelves groaning with preserves and pickles and canned goods, the barns stuffed with hay. He spoke of the health of the community, the new babies born pink and squalling into loving arms, the elderly cared for with tenderness, the sick tended. He spoke of his twins: safely delivered, even though a little early, and a little noisy (everyone laughed), and his wife, Nance, recovering after the emergency lifesaving operation. *Gott* was gut.

Then his tone deepened, growing more contemplative, more personal.

"We give thanks not only for abundance," he intoned, his eyes, sharp and kind in equal measure, moving slowly over the faces before him like a shepherd counting his flock, "but for the trials that teach us our true dependence. Not on our own strength—which fails—but on Gott's grace, which does not. For the wounds—of body, of spirit, of land—that bring forth compassion in others, that remind us we are not solitary creatures but members of a body."

He paused, letting the silence grow heavy with meaning. "For the helpers Gott places in our path, whose skilled hands mend both broken earth and broken bodies, reminding us that we are not meant to bear our burdens alone. That in our weakness, we find the strength of community. That in our need, we discover the gift of others."

Susannah felt her cheeks grow warm, a flush that had nothing to do with the packed barn or the layers of clothing. She kept her eyes demurely on her lap, on her folded hands, but she felt the weight of the Bishop's gaze as it seemed to rest, just for a moment, on various individuals—on Sarah and David Mathews, proof that love could bridge worlds; on John Hostetler, steady and reliable at his forge, always ready to help; on the elderly, like Widow Kaufman, Esther Coblentz, and Ruth, who endured with quiet dignity.

And once, pointedly, his gaze traveled from Nathan, sitting with his injured leg stretched out awkwardly, to Susannah, her healer's hands folded in her lap. It was not an accusation, but it was a *noticing*. A public, if unspoken, acknowledgment. The community's collective awareness of the specific connection between the quiet healer and the injured, solitary farmer was now a fact woven into the fabric of the Thanksgiving sermon, witnessed by all, blessed by implication.

For it was Gott who gave love as surely as the sun and rain.

* * *

After the final, long prayer—spoken in German, each phrase familiar and comforting—the congregation spilled out into the weak, watery November sunlight for a shared meal, a final feast of fellowship before winter's isolation. The change from solemn worship to cheerful community was immediate, voices rising, children freed to run.

Long tables, planks laid on sawhorses, were laden with the women's finest offerings: smoked hams glistening with honey glaze, roasted chickens golden and fragrant, mountains of creamy mashed potatoes, glazed carrots bright as jewels, stewed tomatoes rich with herbs, and every kind of pie imaginable—pumpkin, apple, shoofly, mincemeat—their crusts golden and flaky. The mood was festive, a collective exhalation of relief and gratitude, the hard work done, the winter stores laid in, the community intact.

Susannah was helping Anne Hostetler serve slices of rich, molasses-heavy shoofly pie—the dense, sweet filling like concentrated sunshine against winter's dark—when she felt a solid, familiar presence at her elbow that made her pulse quicken. It was Nathan, leaning on his crutch, a plate in his other hand, his eyes finding hers with an intensity that belied the casual setting.

"You look... well," he said, the simple words freighted with a meaning that vibrated in the space between them, his voice low and private despite the crowd. He looked more at ease than she'd ever seen him in a crowd, as if the public acknowledgment, however subtle, had somehow freed him from the weight of secrecy.

"As do you. The ankle is bearing weight?" she asked, keeping her tone light, clinical, for any nearby ears, though her heart raced.

"Better every day. The healer is skilled." A faint, genuine smile touched his lips, softening the stern line of his mouth, transforming his whole face. "I'm told I might not even have a limp, if I continue to follow orders."

"Then you must continue," she said, allowing herself a small smile in return.

He hesitated, then gestured with a tilt of his head toward a quieter spot near the edge of the woodlot, away from the heart of the chatter and clatter, where the golden leaves lay thick on the ground. "Would you... would you walk with me a short way? The ground is level there by the trees. I'm told the air is... clarifying. *Gut* for the lungs."

It was a bold request, a direct invitation that went beyond medical care. But his injury provided a plausible excuse. A man on a crutch might need a steadying arm, a guide on uneven ground. The community would understand.

She glanced toward her mother, who was deep in conversation with Martha Lapp and Esther Coblentz, a half-eaten piece of pie on her plate, color in her cheeks from the company and the fresh air. Ruth met her daughter's eyes across the crowd and gave a slight, almost imperceptible nod—a blessing, or at least, an acceptance. Permission granted.

"Of course," Susannah said, setting down the pie server. She fell into step beside him, their progress slow and syncopated: the soft *thud* of his crutch, the crunch of her shoes on frozen leaves, their breath visible in the cool air.

* * *

They moved away from the noise, the lively hum of the gathering fading to a distant, pleasant murmur, replaced by the sigh of wind in bare branches and the occasional call of a crow overhead, harsh and lonely. The cold air was indeed clarifying, sharp in their lungs, scented with woodsmoke and earth and the coming winter.

"The Bishop's sermon," Nathan began after they'd walked a ways, then stopped, searching for words as they moved slowly through the dappled shade. "He sees. He knows. The whole community— even the one over in Hope Valley— knows now."

"I know he does," Susannah replied, not looking at him, watching their path, the way the leaves carpeted the ground in shades of amber and rust.

"It doesn't trouble you?" His voice carried genuine concern, worry for her. "The talk it will stir? For you? The speculation, the questions, the pressure?"

Susannah considered, choosing her words with care, knowing this was important. "The talk has always been there, Nathan. About me and Barney—why I hesitate, why I don't accept what everyone says is such a *gut* match. About my mother's health—what will become of me when she passes. About my remedies being old-fashioned, or worse, too close to *Englisch* ways, too much like the superstitions our ancestors left behind."

She paused, stepping over a fallen branch. "People talk. It is the way of a small community. We are known to each other, and that knowing comes with judgment, with opinion. But they also *see*. They see true things, if we are honest. They saw me help you with the plow. They see me caring for my mother day and night. They will see what we choose to show them, consistently, over time. Actions speak louder than rumors."

She stopped walking and turned to face him, her gray eyes direct and unwavering. "What do *you* want to show them, Nathan? What is the truth you want them to see?"

He stopped too, turning to face her, leaning on his crutch, his weight shifted to his good leg. His blue eyes were fierce with a conviction that seemed to burn away the last of his reticence, the last walls crumbling.

"I want to show them a farm that is thriving, not just surviving," he said, his voice low but passionate. "A farm that gives back as much as it takes from the land. That honors the gift of the soil by stewarding it well. I want to show them a man who is faithful, not just to his father's memory and his father's ways, but to Gott's calling for his *own* life—to be a steward who improves what was given him, not just an inheritor who maintains and fears change."

He took a deep, steadying breath, his next words coming slower, weighted with importance. "And I want... I hope, more than I've hoped for anything in a long time... to show them that man standing beside a woman of quiet strength and deep wisdom and gentle kindness. A woman who sees the entire, delicate web of life and isn't afraid to step in and mend its broken threads. A woman who understands that true strength isn't loud or forceful, but patient and knowing."

It was as close to a declaration of intent as he could make in this setting, without the formal, preliminary steps of involving the deacon or the Bishop in an official courtship. It was a promise, raw and sincere, a vision of a shared future offered not with flowers or poetry, but with the profound language of partnership and purpose.

Tears, bright and sudden, blurred her vision, crystallized by the cold air before they could fall, catching on her lashes.

"That," she whispered, her voice thick with emotion she didn't try to hide, "is a future worth waiting for, Nathan King. A future worth building, stone by stone, post by post. A future worth the talk and the trouble and the hard work."

For a moment suspended in time, in the crisp, hushed autumn air with the golden light filtering through the bare branches in shafts like blessings, it was just the two of them and the tangible, shared vision of that future—a farm in balance, a life in partnership, a love rooted in mutual respect and a common dream. The world around them faded to insignificance.

*　*　*

The moment was shattered by the sound of someone clearing their throat, a deliberate, jarring noise that cut through their private world like an axe. Barney Stoltzfus stood a few yards away on the path, his hands thrust into the pockets of his good black coat, his expression carefully neutral, but his posture tense as a drawn bowstring, his shoulders rigid.

"Nathan. Susannah," he said, his voice pleasantly

modulated but hollow, like a bell with no clapper, like words spoken by rote with no feeling behind them. "Enjoying the air? It's brisk. Winter coming on fast." He took a step closer, his boots crunching on leaves. "Nathan, I'm glad to see you on your feet again, if unsteady. We were all concerned."

He paused, then continued, his tone shifting to something that carried the faintest edge of criticism masked as concern. "I was just telling Bishop Miller how we all need to be more mindful with equipment before winter sets in hard. A moment's inattention can cost a season—or worse. Accidents happen when we're overtired, overextended, trying to do too much alone."

The comment was benign on the surface, even helpful, but its intent was a needle, precisely aimed: to remind them both of Nathan's accident, his momentary failure, his vulnerability, and his dependence on Susannah's care. To diminish what they were building by framing it as necessity born of weakness rather than choice born of connection.

Nathan straightened, his grip tightening on the crutch until his knuckles whitened, the wood creaking slightly under the pressure. His face became a mask of polite reserve, but she could see the muscle jumping in his jaw. "Carefulness is a virtue, *jah*," he said, his voice even but cold. "As is knowing when to ask for help rather than pretending strength we don't have."

"It is," Barney agreed smoothly, his eyes shifting to Susannah, dismissing Nathan entirely. "Your mother was looking for you, Susannah. She seemed a bit tired, a bit pale. The cold is hard on those with weak lungs, as you know better than anyone. I offered to fetch you."

It was a dismissal wrapped in solicitous concern, a reminder of her primary duty and of his own attentiveness to her family's needs—an attentiveness that felt more like a claim than a kindness, more like establishing territory than offering help.

The beautiful, fragile bubble of the moment had been punctured. The vision scattered like leaves in the wind. Reality crashed back in.

"I should go to her," Susannah said, her heart sinking like a stone into cold water. She glanced at Nathan, apology and frustration warring in her eyes.

Nathan nodded, his jaw so tight a muscle flickered visibly. "Of course. Please tell her I asked after her health. Sincerely."

As she turned to leave, Barney immediately fell into step beside her, effortlessly matching her pace, his longer legs eating up the ground, leaving Nathan standing alone under the stark, bare trees, a solitary figure leaning on his crutch, watching them walk away together.

* * *

They walked several steps in silence, the sounds of the gathering growing louder as they approached, before Barney spoke, his voice low and confidential, meant only for her ears.

"He's a proud man, Nathan is," Barney said, as if offering sage, brotherly advice. "And a *gut* farmer, in his own rigid way. I'll give him that—his fences are straight, his fields well-tended. But pride and a hard life, carrying a burden alone like he does..." He shook his head. "It can make a man isolated. Brittle. Closed off."

He glanced at her, his brown eyes sincere. "A woman needs companionship, Susannah. She needs laughter in her home, ease in her days, children playing in the yard. She needs a partner who is present, not just physically, but here." He tapped his temple, then his chest over his heart. "Present in mind and spirit, not lost in work and worry. Not carrying the weight of the world on his shoulders and shutting everyone else out."

It was a compelling argument, reasonably delivered. Barney wasn't wrong—not entirely. Nathan *was* burdened, *was* serious, *did* struggle with the weight he carried. But Barney's understanding was surface-level, missing the depth beneath.

Susannah stopped and turned to him, her patience wearing thin, a line crossed. "A woman needs many things, Barney," she replied, her voice even but firm, carrying clearly in the quiet space between them. "Faithfulness. Shared purpose. A vision that stretches beyond the next harvest or the next comfortable meal. And laughter..." she allowed a small, private smile, thinking of Nathan's rare, transformative grins, the light that filled his eyes when he spoke of his dreams for the land, "laughter can come in many forms. It can be the deep, quiet joy of seeing something grow that you nurtured together. Of watching a dream become real through shared work."

He looked at her, truly looked at her, and for the first time, she saw a flicker of doubt, of dawning realization, in his confident, cheerful eyes. The certainty that had always characterised him wavered. He was realizing, perhaps for the first time, that her heart was not a tidy, fenced field to be easily plowed, planted, and claimed by the most suitable bidder. It was a delicate, complex ecosystem—a wild meadow with its own rules, its own seasons, its own mysterious logic. And it had already, irrevocably, begun to bloom for another.

"I see," he said finally, his tone losing its persuasive warmth, becoming resigned, almost sad, the voice of a man accepting defeat. "Well. The Lord's will be done, I suppose. I hope... I truly hope it brings you the joy you seek, Susannah. You deserve that. Every happiness."

He gave a short, polite nod, a gesture of farewell and

surrender, and walked back toward the crowd with purpose, his shoulders set straight but with a defeated slope she hadn't seen before. A good man, accepting that he was not the right man. Not for her.

* * *

The ride home with her mother in the fading light was quiet, the buggy blanket tucked around them both against the chill, their horse's hooves clip-clopping a steady rhythm. As they neared their lane, the familiar outlines of their farm buildings dark silhouettes against the lavender sky, Ruth spoke, her voice frail but clear as a bell in the quiet.

"Nathan King spoke with me briefly today, while you were fetching pie for Esther," she said, not looking at Susannah but straight ahead at the road, at the gathering dusk. "He asked, very properly and with genuine feeling, after my health. Wondered if the frost was bothering my chest, if the cold air in the barn had been too much for me."

She paused, a soft, dry cough escaping her, shaking her thin frame. "But his eyes, Susannah... while his mouth was asking one question about my health, his eyes were asking a different one. A deeper one. A question about my daughter. About my blessing. About whether a certain door might be opened, if he knocked properly."

Susannah's heart leapt to her throat, beating wildly, making it hard to breathe. She held the reins tighter, the leather cold and real in her hands, anchoring her. "And what did you say, *Mamm*?"

Ruth reached over slowly, her movement deliberate, and took her daughter's hand where it gripped the rein, her skin papery and cool but her grip surprisingly firm. "I told him *mei dochder* has a wise heart that listens to things others miss—the language of plants and animals, the voice

- 91 -

of the land itself. And capable hands that are meant for building, not just mending. Hands that should create, not just repair."

She squeezed gently, her voice dropping. "And I told him that a wise heart cannot be forced onto any path, no matter how smooth or well-intentioned. It can only be gently nurtured and then trusted to find its own way, to follow its own true north. That trying to fence it would kill it."

She coughed again, a shallow, weary sound that spoke of the toll the day had taken. "He is a good man, Susannah. His path is steep, and rocky, and there will be little rest on it. Little ease. But I believe, in my old bones, that he would walk it faithfully, without complaint or resentment. And I believe he would carry you gently in his arms when you grew tired, and value your strength when you could walk beside him. He would be a true partner, not just a provider. One who loves you in a way a man should love a woman."

Tears overflowed Susannah's eyes, tracing warm paths down her cold cheeks, dropping onto their clasped hands. Her mother's blessing, subtle and profound, was the final, necessary thread, weaving her private hope into the family tapestry, making it real and sanctioned. "*Denki*, Mamm," she whispered, her voice choked with emotion. "*Denki*."

"Do not thank me," Ruth whispered, leaning her head wearily against her daughter's shoulder, her weight slight as a bird's. "Thank Gott for planting a seed in what looks like rocky ground. His miracles often start that way—in the least likely soil, in the hardest circumstances. And tend it well, *mei kind*. For winter is coming, hard and long, and all growing things, the hardy and the tender alike, need protection and care against the cold. They need faithful tending."

* * *

They turned into their yard, the buggy lamps casting shaky circles of light on the frozen ground, illuminating the familiar path home.

The Thanksgiving service was over. The season of scarcity, of long nights and inward reflection, was upon them. But within Susannah, held close against the cold like a coal wrapped in cloth, she carried a harvest of hope more abundant and sustaining than any cellar full of grain or pantry stocked with preserves.

The balance of her life was shifting, tipping toward a new center of gravity. The torn web of her lonely heart was mending, stronger at the broken places, woven with new threads of silver and gold. And for the first time in her life, she faced the coming deep cold not with dread or resignation, but with the quiet, fierce, nurturing warmth of a promise taking root, waiting patiently for spring.

Waiting for the thaw when all things would bloom.

CHAPTER 6
The First Frost

Winter announced its sovereignty not with a gentle, blanketing snow that softened the world's edges, but with a brutal, silver frost that descended in the deep, silent hour before dawn, that liminal time when the world holds its breath between darkness and light. Susannah woke to a world transformed, every blade of grass, every bare branch, every fence wire encased in a brittle, glittering shell that shattered with the faintest touch, turning to diamond dust in the grey light. The air bit with a dry, clean sharpness that seared the lungs and made each breath visible—a small, transient ghost that vanished as quickly as it formed.

It was breathtakingly beautiful and utterly harsh, a clear, unflinching declaration of the trials to come. Nature showing both her artistry and her cruelty in the same crystalline morning.

The cold, sharper than any in recent memory, deeper than any frost they'd had in years, seeped into the old *daadi haus* with a particular vengeance, finding every crack and keyhole, every gap in the old weatherboarding, exploiting every weakness in the structure's aging defenses. Ruth took to her bed with a finality that frightened Susannah, the rattling cough in her chest tightening into a painful, wheezing knot that seemed to constrict her very being, making each breath a battle won by inches.

The herbal steam Susannah prepared—eucalyptus gathered last summer, pine needles from the woods, and thyme from her own garden—seemed to offer only momentary relief, the warm, medicinal vapor curling into the chill air before the relentless cold reclaimed the room like a conquering army. Fear, a cold of its own making, began to coil tightly in Susannah's stomach, a constant companion as she moved from stove to bedside and back again, her world narrowing to this cycle of care and worry.

She slept in a chair by her mother's bed most nights, dozing fitfully, waking at every change in Ruth's breathing, every cough that tore through the silence. The dark circles under her eyes deepened. Her hands grew chapped from constant washing and cold water. Her prayers became simpler, more desperate: *Please. Not yet. Not yet.*

Her visits to Nathan's farm became less frequent, constrained by her mother's urgent need and the treacherous, icy glaze on the roads that made even short trips dangerous. When she did go, wrapped in every layer she owned, her breath frosting the air before her face, the dynamic between them had shifted yet again. The quiet, profound understanding forged during his convalescence was still there, the bedrock of everything. But now it was overlaid with a new, urgent layer of shared concern—for Ruth, yes, but also for each other, for the fragile thing growing between them against the brutal assault of winter.

Nathan no longer needed her medical care. His ankle was healed, leaving only a slight stiffness he ignored with typical stubbornness, though she noticed he favored it slightly when he thought she wasn't looking, a subtle hitch in his gait that spoke of lingering weakness. Yet, he found reasons to bridge the distance between their farms, to maintain the connection when circumstances tried to sever it.

He would be at the fence line splitting wood when she passed on her way to town, his axe rising and falling with steady rhythm, each strike perfectly placed. Or he would have a sack of extra kindling, cut to perfect lengths and neatly stacked, waiting by his gate "for your mother's fire.

The smaller pieces burn quick and hot when the cold is this deep. Better for a sick room." His gestures were practical, but their timing was precise, an unspoken communication that said *I see you. I know you're struggling. I'm here.*

Once, on a day when the sky was the color of old pewter and the wind cut like a knife, he met her on the lonely lane between their properties, his breath pluming in great gusts in the still, iron-cold air. Without a word, he handed her a small jar, its glass faintly warm from being carried in his coat pocket, held close to his body.

She took it, cradling it in her mittened hands, and held it up to the weak light. Inside was rich, golden honey, thick and slow-moving like liquid amber, with a faint, floral aroma that made her think of summer meadows and warm afternoons—things that felt impossibly distant now.

"From my hives," he said simply, his voice roughened by cold. "The last extraction of the season. The lavender field ones." He'd remembered her mentioning the lavender in her salve, that detail from weeks ago. The gift was practical—honey was excellent for a sore throat, everyone knew that—but its intention was deeply personal, a thread of attentive care woven directly from the heart of his world to the heart of hers.

"*Denki*, Nathan," she said, her fingers closing around the jar, absorbing its residual warmth like a benediction. "She will appreciate it. Mamm always says the sweetness helps when the medicines are bitter. Makes them easier to bear."

He nodded, his gaze searching her face with an intensity that made her feel exposed, vulnerable, seeing the new shadows of sleepless nights under her eyes, the tightness around her mouth that spoke of constant worry, the slight tremor in her hands that came from exhaustion and fear.

"You carry it alone," he stated, not as a question but as a recognized fact, spoken with the certainty of someone who understood that particular burden intimately. "The worry, the watching, the work. It's a heavy load for one pair of shoulders. Too heavy."

"It is my place," she replied automatically, but her voice wavered, betraying the strain, the near-breaking point she was approaching. "My duty. What *dochder* would not—"

"A shared burden is lighter," he interrupted quietly, his words hanging in the frozen air like a visible thing, substantial. The implication was clear and profound. He was not offering empty comfort or fleeting help or the kind of sympathy that evaporated like morning frost. He was offering a partnership that extended beyond dreams of fertile pastures and companion planting to the hard, cold, unglamorous reality of a sickroom and a weary heart. It was a deeper vow than any about crops or soil; it was a vow about the soil of their lives, about walking through the valleys as well as celebrating on the hilltops.

"I know," she whispered, her eyes stinging with tears that the cold froze before they could fall. "I know, Nathan."

The community, meanwhile, was busy with its own winter preparations—butchering hogs, smoking meat, endless baking of cookies and breads to fill pantries against the lean months. Yet the undercurrent of speculation about Susannah Mast and Nathan King did not freeze with the pond behind the old schoolhouse. If anything, it intensified, flourished in the warm, steamy kitchens during quilting bees, and around the pot-bellied stove at the harness shop where the men gathered. The story had taken on a life of its own: the healing woman and the solitary farmer, the injured ankle, the faithful visits, the honey given.

Barney Stoltzfus, ever present, ever amiable, seemed to

redouble his respectful, visible attentions, as if making a public case before an invisible jury. He brought a bottle of cherry-red *Englisch* cough syrup to Ruth, "from the pharmacy in town—very modern, the pharmacist says it works wonders," a deliberate contrast to Nathan's homespun, amber honey. He offered, loudly and in front of others at the general store, to chop their entire winter woodpile, a gallant, sweeping gesture that drew approving nods from the older women.

"*Denki*, Barney, but a neighbor has already seen to it," Susannah had replied politely, not naming the neighbor as being Nathan but not wishing to lie either. "Very kind of you to offer."

"Ah, of course," Barney had said, his smile not faltering, though something flickered in his eyes—disappointment, or perhaps frustration. "Well, if Nathan King is too busy with his own spread to help, you know I am always happy to lend my strength. A woman shouldn't have to rely on distant neighbors when closer help is available."

The jab was subtle, questioning Nathan's ability to provide, to be present when needed. "We manage fine," she had repeated, her tone leaving no room for further argument, her grey eyes steady and cool. "But I appreciate your concern."

The message was sent and received. She was not accepting courtship from that quarter. Her path, rocky as it was, had been chosen, and she would not be swayed by offers of easier roads and warmer hearths.

* * *

The crisis came on a night when the wind screamed around the eaves of the little *daadi haus* like a tormented thing, rattling the windows in their frames with such violence that Susannah feared the glass would shatter. The sound was primal, terrifying, like all the loneliness and cold in the world given voice.

Ruth's breathing, already ragged and labored, grew shallow and desperate, each inhalation a whistling struggle through a narrowed passage, each exhalation a weak, defeated sigh that seemed to give up a little more life. Her skin was hot and dry as parchment despite the roaring fire Susannah kept fed until the stove glowed dull red and ticked with dangerous heat, the room stifling yet still not warm enough to ease the chill in Ruth's frail bones.

The usual remedies—the steam, the honey stirred into warm milk, the mullein tea—had no effect, useless as stones against this onslaught. A deep, barking cough, unlike any before, seized her frail frame, shaking her violently like a rag doll and leaving her gasping, her eyes wide with a terror that mirrored Susannah's own. The terror of drowning on dry land, of suffocating despite the air, of feeling death's hand close around the throat.

Panic, cold and pure and utterly paralyzing, shot through Susannah like ice water in her veins. And still her mother would not have her call for the *doktor*. The weight of her knowledge felt suddenly insufficient, crushing. She felt utterly, desperately alone, small and helpless before the vast indifference of death. The howling wind was the only answer to her silent, desperate prayers.

Then, through the berserk symphony of the gale, she heard it—not a knock, but a solid, rhythmic *thump-thump-thump* against the door, as if someone were using a heavy fist or a boot, demanding entry. Her heart leaped into her throat.

Wrapping a shawl around her shaking shoulders, she rushed to open it, the wind nearly tearing the door from her grasp when she unlatched it, cold air rushing in like a flood.

Nathan stood on the porch, hatless, his hair wild, covered in a dusting of driven snow that glittered in the lamplight like ground glass, his shoulders hunched against the blasting fury. In his arms was a bulky, canvas-wrapped bundle clutched tight to his chest. His face was grim, etched with determination and cold, his lips nearly blue, but his eyes burned with urgent purpose, with a fierce protectiveness that took her breath away.

"Dr Mathews," he said without preamble, his voice raw and carried almost away by the wind. He didn't wait for invitation; he stepped inside, bringing a swirl of stinging, icy air and the smell of snow and night with him. "I went to him. For your mother. I figured if she would not go to him, he could come to her in his way."

He moved immediately to the table and began unwrapping the bundle with stiff, clumsy fingers. "He said to use what you need. He talked me through it on the ride back—dosages, methods, everything." He held out items with reverent care: a small, modern plastic device with a mouthpiece—an inhaler, utterly alien in the rustic room— and several small bottles with typed labels. "There are antibiotics. And this inhalant, for opening the lungs."

Susannah stared, stunned into silence, her mind struggling to catch up with what this meant. Nathan had done the unthinkable. He had gone to an *Englischer*, to Dr Mathews, in the middle of a raging storm, crossing lines that were rarely crossed, and not just for advice, but for modern, forbidden medicine—the kind that conservative members of the community viewed with deep suspicion. He had risked censure and gossip of the most serious kind, had potentially put his own standing in the community at risk, for *her*. For her mother.

"Whoever wants to can talk to me tomorrow," he said, his jaw set like granite, immovable. His eyes met hers, unwavering, burning with conviction. "Tonight, a life is in the balance. A good woman is suffering. I will not stand by and let her fade because we're afraid of whispers or rules made by men."

He placed the bag and the inhaler gently on the table, his faith in her judgment absolute, a solid rock in her whirling storm of fear. "So use these things. Save her. And I will face whatever comes after."

Tears of relief, of overwhelming, soul-deep gratitude, choked her, closed her throat. There was no time for words, for proper thanks. Ruth's labored breathing pulled her back. She nodded, a quick, sharp movement, and grabbed the bag, her healer's instincts snapping back into focus with laser intensity, armed now with new, potent tools. And once again, in a time of crisis, her heart cried out a loud silent thanks to Gott. The Englisch medicine had saved Nance Miller and her twin sons— her two wonderfully noisy sons. And now, perhaps, it might save Ruth.

* * *

The next hours were a blur of measured desperation, lit by the frantic dance of lamplight that threw wild shadows on the walls.

She helped her mother with the strange inhaler, coaching her through weak, desperate breaths, her voice calm and encouraging even as her own heart raced. "That's it, Mamm. Breathe in slowly. Hold it. Good. Again." She held the plastic contraption—so foreign, so *Englisch*—with a reverence she usually reserved for prayer, because in this moment, it *was* prayer made tangible.

Her mother, fear filling her face, conceded, even swallowing the antibiotics, the first *Englisch* pills she had ever taken in her life. Nobody was forcing *Englisch* medicine on Ruth against her will: much as they wanted her to have it. Susannah wondered that perhaps hearing Bishop Miller's testimony at thanksgiving about Gott's hand in his wife's labor had softened something in Ruth. If so, *praise Gott for Bishop Miller.*

The old ways, Susannah realized with a new force, had their place alongside the new ways, neither replacing each other. The two together were a God-given path to healing. And now, because Nathan had come with the *Englischer* way, Gott could do His healing work in Ruth.

Nathan did not leave. He stoked the fire until the stove glowed cherry-red, unsafe but necessary. He melted snow in pots for water, brought fresh cloths from the cupboard, and sat in the shadows of the kitchen corner, a silent, steadfast presence. He didn't speak, didn't interfere, didn't get in the way. His mere being there, solid and unshakeable as bedrock, kept the terror at bay. He was sharing the burden, just as he'd promised. Just as she had once his. Just by being there, by refusing to leave her alone in this dark vigil.

Slowly, agonizingly slowly, like ice melting under reluctant spring sun, the crisis broke. The choking tightness in Ruth's chest began to ease, the terrifying whistle in her breath softening to a rasp, then to something closer to normal breathing. The fever broke into a drenching, exhausted sweat that soaked the sheets but signaled the body winning its war. Her breathing, while still weak and uneven, found a ragged, steady rhythm that Susannah recognized as the sound of life persisting, of crisis passing.

Spent, Ruth fell into a deep, natural sleep, her face finally relaxing from its mask of pain and struggle, looking more peaceful than she had in weeks.

* * *

Dawn was a faint, grey leaching of the black from the sky, more absence of dark than presence of light, when Susannah finally stepped out of the sickroom. Her body trembled with fatigue, her dress stained with sweat and herbs and the evidence of battle. Nathan was still there, sitting at the scrubbed wooden table, his head bowed in his hands, elbows on the scarred surface. He looked up as she entered, his face drawn with his own exhaustion, shadowed with beard, but his eyes were immediately alert, searching hers.

"She sleeps," Susannah whispered, her voice raw and cracked from hours of speaking encouragement, from breathing steam, from praying aloud. "The fever is gone. She breathes easier. The... the medicine worked. You saved her life, Nathan."

She gazed heavenwards for a moment, thanking Gott with outspread palms for doing His healing work, whether than was through herbs, antibiotics and inhalers, or literal signs and wonders. *All were miracles.*

"Denki, Herr Gott… You pulled *Maam* out of the pit and out from the muddy mire." The words she quoted were from Psalm 40, one they sometimes sang at church.

Then, after thanking Gott, Suzannah's eyes flicked back to Nathan. He had uttered an amen and his straw hat was in his hands.

The relief that washed over his face was so profound it seemed to soften every hard line, making him look suddenly younger, vulnerable. He stood awkwardly, as if to go, but swayed slightly with weariness. He had been awake all night, after a long day's work, after a risky, freezing journey through the storm to Noah's and back, miles in brutal conditions.

"You should rest," she said, her voice gentle despite her own exhaustion. "Here. Before you go back out into the cold. Just for a little while."

He shook his head, gathering his resolve like a cloak around him. "I'll go. The talk will be bad enough without me being found here at dawn. That would be a burden on you I didn't intend to bring. Your reputation—"

But she moved to the stove, cutting off his protest, pouring the last of the hot water from the kettle into a cup, her hands shaking slightly. "Tea, first. Please." It was a plea, not just for him to drink, but for him to stay a moment longer in the sanctuary they had created together this terrible, sacred night—a sanctuary of shared purpose and silent, potent love.

He accepted the cup, their fingers touching, the contact sending warmth through her cold hands. The silence now was dense, filled with all that had passed—the fear, the risk, the unwavering support, the miracle of a life pulled back from the edge.

"You could be shunned by some," she said, the words a pained whisper, voicing the fear that had gnawed at her all night beneath the more immediate terror. "For what you did. For going to Dr Mathews, for bringing these *Englisch* medicines. It's a direct challenge to the old ways. The conservative families will demand—"

He met her gaze, his blue eyes clear and unafraid in the cold, grey morning light filtering through the window, catching the exhaustion but also the absolute certainty.

"Susannah," he said, his voice low and firm, brooking no argument. "Some lines the community draws are in sand, shifted by the wind of need and circumstance. Some are drawn in stone, never to be moved. Letting a good woman suffer, letting a daughter watch her mother fade when help was possible, for the sake of a line drawn in sand... that is not faithfulness to Gott. That is fear of man. That is pride masquerading as piety."

He took a sip of the bitter tea, grimacing slightly, then continued. "I was afraid tonight. More afraid than I've been since my own mother passed. But not of being shunned. I was afraid *for* you. Afraid of watching you bear this terrible weight alone, with your good heart breaking. That fear... that love..." He paused, letting the word hang there, spoken aloud for the first time. "That love was stronger than any other fear. And if following love means facing the community's questions, then I will face them gladly."

It was the most eloquent, heartfelt speech she had ever heard him make. He had acted not in defiance of his faith, but in accordance with its deepest, truest law—the law of mercy, of compassion in action, of love demonstrated through sacrifice. It was the same law that had guided her to help him with his plow, that guided her hands with her herbs, that made her see the suffering in a frightened horse. They were, in this fundamental way, mirrors of each other. Two faithful hearts, interpreting their duty through the lens of love rather than fear.

"You saved her life," she said again, the tears coming freely now, hot against her cold cheeks. "You risked everything—"

"*We* did," he corrected firmly, without a hint of false modesty, his voice strong and certain. "With David Mathews' tools, and your wisdom, and..." He hesitated, the word still new and powerful on his tongue, still frightening in its implications. "And because we were not alone. We did it together. That's what partnership means, Susannah. Sharing the impossible burdens. Making them possible. With Gott's help."

We. The word hung in the quiet, dawn-lit kitchen, solid and real as the table between them, as substantial as the crisis they had just weathered together. It was no longer a hopeful concept, a fragile possibility spoken in fields and sick rooms. It was a fact, forged in the night's desperate fire, proven under pressure, tempered by trial.

He left as the first weak, milky sun tried to penetrate the thick frost on the windows, painting everything in shades of pearl and silver. Susannah watched from the door as his broad back disappeared down the lane, his footsteps leaving dark, purposeful prints in the pristine, crystalline white. The world outside was still frozen, still harsh and unyielding, winter tightening its grip. But something had thawed deep within her, a final, lingering doubt about his heart, about the depth of his commitment, melted away by the fierce, sacrificial heat of his actions. The ice on the branches might glitter with brittle beauty, but a stronger fire now burned in her soul, warming her from within.

***

The gossip, when it came, was swift and sharp as the frost itself. Nathan King had been seen at the Mathews place in the worst of the storm, a reckless journey no sane man would make without dire cause. He had been seen carrying an *Englisch* medical bag. Whispers became murmurs, murmurs became pointed questions asked in concerned tones that barely masked judgment. *Was he turning to the outside world? Rejecting the community's ways? Setting a dangerous precedent?*

Bishop Lapp summoned him within two days, the message delivered by the Bishop's youngest son with appropriate solemnity. While David Mathews was the Bishop's son-in-law, David—and his wife, Sarah— straddled a fine line between both worlds that met critique, and sometime misunderstanding, even from their own family. And this was despite Nance Miller's testimony. The truth is Englisch medicine was more *tolerated* than it was welcomed. But toleration was better than outright rejected.

Susannah waited in an agony of suspense, tending to her slowly, miraculously recovering mother—Ruth who sat up in bed now, who took broth without choking, who smiled weakly when Susannah read scripture to her. Each hour stretched like taffy, elastic with anxiety.

When Susannah saw Nathan's buggy turn into his lane late that afternoon, she could wait no longer. She wrapped a shawl around herself and walked through the biting cold to the fence line where it had all begun months ago with a broken plow—that first thread of connection that had pulled them together.

He was in the barn, forking hay down to the waiting stock, his movements strong and restored, no sign of the exhausted man from two nights before. He saw her through the barn door and came out immediately, leaning the pitchfork against the doorframe, his expression serious but not defeated.

"The Bishop?" she asked without preamble, her breath a swift white cloud between them, her heart hammering.

Nathan leaned against the barn siding, crossing his arms against the cold, his face thoughtful. "He asked for the truth. I gave it to him. All of it. I told him of your mother's need, of my choice, of David's help without which she might have died. I didn't hide anything or make excuses."

He paused, his gaze steady on hers. "He was quiet for a long time. You could hear the clock tick in that front room, hear the fire settling. Then he said..." Nathan's voice dropped, taking on the measured cadence of the Bishop's speech. "'The letter of the law kills, but the spirit gives life. You acted in the spirit of compassion, which is the heart of all law. To save a life is a sacred duty, Nathan King. Even our Lord healed on the Sabbath, breaking the letter to honor the spirit.'"

Susannah let out a breath she didn't know she was

holding, her shoulders sagging with relief. "Then... he approved?"

"He understood," Nathan corrected carefully.

Nathan's expression grew more serious. He then told Susannah what Bishop Lapp had apparently really wanted to talk to him about, repeating the bishop's words verbatim: "'Your intentions toward the Mast woman are now clear to all who have eyes. If they are serious, they must be made proper and public, through the church, to remove any shadow of scandal or confused allegiance. Clarity protects everyone—you, her, the community. What is hidden breeds speculation. What is open and blessed can be defended.'"

Susannah's heart hammered against her ribs, a wild, hopeful drum. "What did you say?"

A slow, sure smile, the first truly easy, unburdened one she had ever seen from him, spread across his face, lighting his eyes from within like sunrise breaking over frozen fields. "I said my intentions were very serious. That they were rooted in respect and shared faith and a vision for a life of partnership. And that I would speak to Elder Yoder this very week, so that my courtship of Susannah Mast could be published with the church's blessing, for all to see and know. No more shadows. No more whispers. Just the truth, spoken plain."

The world seemed to tilt, the frost-dusted fields blurring into a shimmer of gold in the late afternoon light. It was happening. Not in secret, not in stolen moments by fences or in sickrooms, but openly, properly, with the Bishop's challenging but ultimately approving nod. The community's watchful eyes would now see a blessed path, not a secret scandal. The thread that had been woven between them in private would now be displayed for all, woven into the larger tapestry of their community's life.

"Nathan..." she began, but words failed, overwhelmed,

lost in the swell of joy that threatened to overflow.

He reached out, not to touch her—they were still visible from the road, still bound by propriety—but to point past her, toward the west pasture, now sleeping under its thick white blanket. "The ground is frozen hard now. Locked tight like iron. But beneath, the clover seeds we talked about, they wait in the dark. The roots of the old grass are gathering strength where we can't see them, preparing."

His eyes returned to hers, holding her with the certainty of the changing seasons, with the faith of a farmer who plants in fall trusting spring will come. "Our season of waiting is over, Susannah. The frost did its work. When the thaw comes, we will build our dream. Together. In the clear light of day, with the whole community watching. With their blessing."

He didn't ask her. He declared it, with the same steadfast faith with which he planted a crop, trusting the sun and the rain and the good earth to do their part while he did his. And she knew, with every fiber of her being, that she would stand beside him in that field when spring came, her hand in his, their shared purpose as real as the thawing soil beneath their feet.

The first, hardest frost had passed. What lay ahead was the long, quiet, nurturing work of winter—tending the hidden, promised life waiting below the frozen surface. But spring would come. It always did. And they would face it together.

CHAPTER 7
Love in Bloom

The old *dawdi haus* on the King farm, which had once been a place of convalescence and hushed, life-altering conversations, now hummed with a new, vibrant life that transformed every corner, every shadow. For Susannah, stepping across its threshold as Nathan's wife on a bright, cold December afternoon was not an entry into a stranger's space, but a homecoming to a shell that had been waiting, patient and empty, to be filled with their shared breath, their shared silence, their shared dreams.

The threshold itself felt significant—a literal crossing from one life to another. She paused there for just a moment, Nathan's hand warm on her elbow, and looked back at the gathered community still lingering in the farmyard after the wedding festivities, their faces bright with cold and fellowship. Then she turned forward, toward the small house that was now *theirs*, and stepped inside to begin.

The wedding itself had been a blur of solemn joy, a day that felt both endless and over in a heartbeat—the long service in the Bishop's home, three hours of hymns and sermons and ancient words, her hand trembling slightly in Nathan's steady grasp as they took their vows before Gott and community. The weight of those promises had settled on her shoulders like a mantle—heavy, but in the way that important things are heavy, grounding rather than crushing.

The shared meal afterward had been filled with well-wishes that seemed to coat them like a tangible blessing. Bishop and Nance Miller's babies wailed but even that baby noise felt like a loud and fitting testimony to Gott's hand at work in all their lives.

Ruth, wrapped in a new shawl Susannah had woven for her in shades of deep blue—strong enough now to attend, to witness, to give her blessing with tears streaming down her pale cheeks—had smiled a smile of such profound peace that it eased any lingering ache in Susannah's heart. Her mother had lived to see this day. That alone felt like a miracle.

The celebrations had ended as the sun began its early winter descent, the last of the leftover roast chicken and pumpkin pie consumed by visiting relatives who had traveled from neighboring districts. The community's good wishes still seemed to linger in the crisp winter air like the scent of woodsmoke and fresh-baked bread, a blessing that would carry them through the hard months ahead.

Now, it was just the two of them, Ruth nearby, and the vast, silent farm sleeping under a deep quilt of snow. The world narrowed to this: four walls, a glowing stove, and the enormity of beginning a life together.

Three Years Later

The west pasture was no longer a place of rocky struggle and stubborn despair, no longer the barren, broken ground that had tested Nathan's father and defeated his spirit. It had become instead a testament to a promise kept, a living psalm of faithfulness sung in green and gold. Where Nathan had once wrestled with rotten posts and unyielding ground, cursing the stones that broke plow blades and the thin soil that grew more thistles than grass, a gentle slope now lay cloaked in a lush, undulating carpet of white and crimson clover that moved in the breeze like a living sea, buzzing with the drowsy, contented industry of thousands of bees—Nathan's hives, carefully placed and faithfully tended.

Along the repaired southern fence line, the dwarf apple

and pear trees they had planted with their own hands stood as young, confident sentinels, no longer the fragile saplings they'd staked and watered through that first anxious summer. Their branches were adorned with the delicate, hopeful blossoms of early May, a confetti of pink and white against the clear blue sky that seemed to celebrate existence itself. At their feet, just as Susannah had envisioned years ago by a cold fire in the lee of a wagon, a riot of lavender and scarlet bee balm softened the tree lines, their spiky blooms a vibrant, fragrant tapestry that shifted and danced in the breeze, attracting butterflies and hummingbirds alongside the bees.

In the very center of this transformed field, on a beloved old quilt spread over the soft clover—a wedding gift from Esther Yoder, its pattern called "Wedding Ring," each stitch a prayer—Susannah sat with a baby girl asleep in the curve of her arm. Little Esther—named after her mother's wise friend, just six months old, had her father's fair, downy hair that caught the sunlight like spun gold, and her mother's serious, observing gray eyes, which even in sleep seemed to be dreaming deep infant dreams of wonder and mystery.

Nearby, three-year-old David—named after the Englisch doktor who had saved his *grossmammi*—was "helping" his father check the new drip irrigation lines for the raspberry and blueberry bushes they'd added that spring. He was a miniature of Nathan in his tiny straw hat and earnest expression, his chubby hands getting in the way more than assisting, but Nathan's patience was infinite, explaining each connection, each valve, as if speaking to a fellow farmer rather than a toddler.

"See here?" Nathan said, crouching down to David's level, his large hand guiding the small one to feel the water flowing through the line. "The water goes where the roots need it. Not wasted on the top where it dries in the sun.

Smart farming. Working *with* how Gott made things, not against it."

"Smart," mini David repeated solemnly, nodding with grave, comical understanding, his little face scrunched in concentration.

Susannah watched them, her heart a slow, steady drum of deep, rooted contentment that seemed to pulse in time with the earth itself. The scene was a prayer made visible, an answered petition she hadn't even known how to voice three years ago when she'd been a lonely girl tending herbs and a sick mother, her future a grey uncertainty. David's high, chattering questions—a joyful mix of Pennsylvania Dutch and the Englisch words he picked up from 'Uncle' David, his much loved namesake—were met with Nathan's low, patient answers, never dismissive, always explaining, treating the boy's curiosity as sacred. Little David would even play dress up at being a *doktor* and it made Susannah's heart glad.

Nathan would pause, point at a blossom on a young apple tree, and say something about bees and pollination and fruit that made David nod with that wonderful, serious expression children get when they think they're learning important grown-up secrets. This was the laughter and ease Barney Stoltzfus had once spoken of— not the light, social kind found at singings and frolics, but the deep, joyful, often quiet kind that sprang from shared purpose, shared work, and a love that had been tested in winter storms and sickrooms and proven true.

Barney himself was married now, to a cheerful, capable girl named Rachel from Hope Valley with a ready laugh and skilled hands, her quilts already winning ribbons at the county fair. They had a rosy-cheeked baby boy of their own, and Barney's farm flourished in its orderly, prosperous way. At church, he would give Susannah and Nathan a friendly, genuine nod across the room, the old rivalry and hurt softened by time and his own happiness into a mutual respect within the tight, forgiving weave of community. He had found his joy on his smooth, well-tended path; she had found hers here, among the rocks and the clover, in the arms of a quiet man who showed love through actions rather than words.

Nathan finished his task and scooped up a squealing David with easy strength, settling him effortlessly on his broad shoulders as he walked back to the quilt, the boy's delighted laughter ringing across the field like bells. He lowered his large frame beside Susannah with a quiet sigh of pure satisfaction, the sound of a man who has found his place in the world and knows it. He didn't speak immediately, just reached out a calloused, gentle finger to trace the downy curve of Esther's cheek, so soft it seemed impossible that the world could contain such delicacy.

The look on Nathan's face—a mixture of awe, fierce protectiveness, and a profound, settled peace—was one Susannah knew she would never tire of seeing, would carry in her heart until her last breath. It was the face of a man who had found his balance, who had learned that strength came not from carrying everything alone but from sharing the load with a true partner.

"The clover took better than I ever hoped," he said finally, his voice a quiet rumble of contentment, satisfaction earned through years of patient work. He gazed out over the blooming field, his eyes seeing simultaneously the past struggle and the present bounty, the vision and its fulfillment. "The soil's improving—you can smell it. Richer, deeper. Earthworms everywhere, which means the soil is alive again. Next year, I think we might try a patch of butternut squash in that far corner, where the ground's been resting. The vines will cover the ground, keep the weeds down, and the bees will help with pollination."

"And the lavender at the edges will keep the squash bugs away," Susannah added, leaning her head against his solid shoulder, breathing in the scent of sun-warmed cotton, soil, and him—a scent that meant home and safety and belonging. "It's all connected. Just like Grossmammi said. Everything has its place, its purpose, its partner."

"*Jah*," he said, the word full of a rich, hard-won satisfaction that came from seeing a dream become reality through sweat and faith. He looked at her, his blue eyes clear and bright in the golden afternoon light. "Like us."

Their home had been expanded two years prior—a proper bedroom added upstairs under the eaves for the children, with two windows that caught the morning sun and evening breezes. A larger, sunlit kitchen now housed Susannah's growing still-room in a dedicated alcove, with shelves from floor to ceiling. Her small but thriving business of dried herbs, tinctures, and salves had grown beyond anything she'd imagined, sought after even in neighboring districts and by *Englisch* customers who came on recommendation, willing to pay for quality and knowledge.

She'd learned to navigate the balance between tradition and practicality, always careful to frame her work as simple folk remedies, never claiming more than was proper, always directing serious ailments to doctors while offering comfort for minor complaints. The income wasn't substantial, but it was steady, and more importantly, it was hers—her contribution to their partnership, valued and respected.

Ruth had lived to see the first delicate apple blossoms adorn the young trees, to hold her granddaughter Esther with trembling, joyful hands, tears streaming down her face as she whispered prayers of thanksgiving. She had passed peacefully the previous winter on a snowy afternoon, her hand in Susannah's, her last words a whispered, "*Gott sei Dank. Denki, mei liewe kind.*" My garden... is in such good hands." The legacy of healing had been passed, and it flourished in Susannah's capable hands and would someday pass to Esther if God willed it. And David too, perhaps following the path of his 'uncle'.

The funeral had been well-attended, the community gathering to honor a quiet woman who had raised a daughter of wisdom and compassion. Nathan had stood beside Susannah throughout, his hand on her back, his presence a steady anchor as she navigated her grief. In the weeks after, he'd taken over more of the household tasks without being asked, giving her space to mourn while ensuring she wasn't alone in her sorrow.

Nathan's farm was not the largest in the district, nor the most prosperous in conventional terms, but it was becoming known as one of the most resilient, innovative, and oddly fruitful—a place where old wisdom and new methods met and married. His partnership with Dr David Mathews had deepened into an unlikely but powerful alliance that benefited the entire community—Nathan's deep, traditional knowledge and relentless work ethic paired seamlessly with David's scientific understanding and unwavering respect for Plain ways.

They consulted on livestock health and soil management, David often bringing agricultural extension pamphlets and research papers, David and Nathan translating them together, seeking practical applications that worked within the Ordnung. Their friendship was a quiet, sturdy bridge between worlds that served and strengthened the whole community, proving that faithfulness to tradition and openness to wisdom could coexist.

As the afternoon sun warmed the blossoming field, painting everything in shades of honey and gold, Sarah Mathews came walking up the lane, carrying a basket that gave off the unmistakable, sugary scent of fresh baking, still warm from her oven.

"I come bearing blackberry pie," she called, her smile as warm as the sunshine, her hazel eyes bright with affection and mischief. Behind her, David followed, his outsider status long since forgotten by Nathan and Susannah, if not by others in Miracle Creek.

They made a picnic of it right there in the pasture, the families mingling with the easy comfort of long friendship. Long tables weren't needed; quilts spread on clover served just as well. The children tumbled and giggled in the soft clover, chasing fat bumblebees—carefully, having learned the hard way about consequences—and picking flowers to weave into chains.

Sarah's eyes, wise and kind and knowing, sparkled as she took in the blooming rows, the healthy trees, the general aura of peace and prosperity that hung over the field like a benediction. "David says the agricultural extension agent from the college was out here last week," she mentioned casually, slicing the pie with precise movements, the purple filling rich and gleaming. "He was asking all about this place. Called it a 'model of sustainable, small-scale polyculture' or some such fancy term. He wanted to know who the farmer was behind it, wanted to interview Nathan for some publication."

Nathan snorted softly, a familiar, amused sound that meant he was pleased but would never admit it, but a hint of quiet, justified pride touched his eyes—pride not in himself, but in what the land had become. "He can call it what he likes in his big words. I just call it good sense. And faithfulness to the land. Working with Gott's design instead of fighting it."

"And to each other," Susannah added softly, her hand finding Nathan's on the quilt between them, their fingers intertwining naturally, automatically, the way breathing happened—necessary and unconsidered. Their wedding bands—simple, unadorned gold—caught the sunlight.

"Amen to that," David said with feeling, his arm around Sarah's shoulders. "That's the real secret. The partnership. The rest is just technique."

Later, after their friends had left and the children, exhausted by sun and play and too much pie, were dozing on the quilt like puppies in a pile, Nathan and Susannah packed up their little domain with the practiced efficiency of long partnership. He carried Esther, a precious bundle against his chest, her head on his shoulder, drool dampening his shirt collar. Susannah held David's sleepy hand, the boy stumbling and yawning as they walked slowly back toward the house, their shadows long and intertwined in the golden, honeyed light of late afternoon.

They paused at the crest of the hill, as was their habit —a ritual that had developed over the years, this moment of looking back and taking stock, of witnessing what had been built. They looked back over the west pasture, and the sight never failed to move Susannah, to bring tears of gratitude to her eyes.

The field was awash in the glow of the setting sun, the white clover like a sea of tiny, luminous stars, the young fruit trees casting long, peaceful shadows that stretched like reaching hands. It was a picture of abundance, not of mere quantity, but of health, balance, and a dream patiently, stubbornly, lovingly nurtured into reality through seasons of doubt and seasons of plenty.

"Do you ever think of it?" Nathan asked quietly, his voice barely more than a breath in the still air, not wanting to wake the children. "That first day, with the broken plow? How different it all could have been if you'd just walked on by? If you'd been too proper, too cautious, to offer help to a stranger?"

Susannah looked from the blooming field that was their

shared heart's work, the fruit of their partnership made visible, to her husband's profile, now etched with lines of strength and quiet joy instead of solitary strain, weathered by sun and wind but softened by love. Then down at their sleeping children, their greatest, most vulnerable harvest, their most precious fruit. She thought of the lonely girl she had been, tending her herbs and her mother, her heart a fallow field, her future a grey question mark.

She thought of the isolated man he had been, fighting his rocky soil and his father's ghost, his heart a sealed chamber, his days measured in duty rather than joy. She thought of the storms weathered, both outside and in— the blizzard that had tested their newborn partnership, the fears shared and conquered, the grief and celebrations witnessed together. She thought of the life they had built not on ease, but on meaning, on a promise made over a broken tool and kept through determination and grace.

"I think," she said, her voice clear and sure in the tender twilight, full of the wisdom of one who has walked through fire and found gold in the ashes, "that Gott in His wisdom does not always steer us to the easy road, but to the right one. The one meant for our souls. The one that shapes us into who we're meant to become."

She turned to him, her gray eyes shining with love and certainty that had only deepened with time and trial. "The plow broke so we could meet. The pasture was rocky so we could learn to mend it together, to create something new rather than repeating what had failed. The winter was hard so we could appreciate the depth of this spring and every spring after."

She squeezed his hand. "I would not change a single stone in that field, Nathan. Not one. For every stone, every struggle, every moment of doubt led us right here. To this moment. To these *kinner.* To this life we built together from nothing but vision and faith."

He turned to her, his blue eyes shining with unshed tears that reflected the glorious sky painted in rose and violet and gold. He leaned down carefully, mindful of the sleeping baby in his arms, and kissed her, not with the fiery spark of their first touch years ago, but with a gentle, lasting promise that tasted of honey and clover and home and forever.

"My Susannah," he murmured against her lips, the words a cherished prayer worn smooth by repetition but never losing their power. "My wise heart. My greatest harvest. My partner in all things."

"And you are mine," she whispered back, her free hand coming up to cup his bearded cheek, feeling the warmth of his skin, the solidness of him. "My rock. My shelter. My home."

Hand in hand, with their children safe between them, they turned toward the warm, lit windows of their home, where the evening lamp had just been lit by Aunt Edna, who still lived in the main house and helped with the children, her face kind and accepting where it had once been merely tolerant. Behind them, over the west pasture now tinged with purple dusk, the first fireflies of the season emerged, their tiny, miraculous lights winking on and off like a thousand silent, blinking blessings in the gathering night, like stars come down to earth to celebrate the day's ending.

The story of the farmer and the healer was no longer just a courtship or a romance whispered about at quilting bees. It was simply their life—a life of predawn prayers whispered side-by-side in the grey hour before sunrise, of hard work that satisfied the soul more than any leisure, of dreams shared over seed catalogs and sickbeds, of a love as deep, as nurturing, and as fertile as the good soil they tended together.

It was a life of quiet, extraordinary blessings, sown in faith and watered with tears and laughter, pruned by hardship and allowed to flourish in the sun of grace, now blooming in the gentle, enduring light of a Pennsylvania evening that promised another dawn, and another after that, stretching into a future they would face together.

And it was, they knew with every shared breath, with every glance at the sleeping children and the thriving field, with every simple meal eaten together at their kitchen table, with every challenge met and overcome, only the beginning. The best fruit, Nathan often said, takes years to develop. Their love was still young, still growing, still reaching toward the light.

As they reached the porch steps, David stirred in Susannah's arms and murmured sleepily, "Dat? When can I help plant the squash?"

Nathan's face lit with that transformative smile, the one that still made Susannah's heart skip even after three years of marriage. "In the spring, *bu*. When the ground is warm. We'll do it together."

"Together," David echoed, satisfied, and slipped back into sleep.

Susannah caught Nathan's eye over the children's heads, and they shared a look of perfect understanding, of deep contentment, of gratitude for the simple and the profound all woven together. Together. It was the word that defined them, the principle that had carried them from a broken plow in an autumn field to this moment of peace and plenty.

Together, they had taken rocky ground and made it fertile. Together, they had weathered storms and celebrated harvests. Together, they had built a life worth living, a love worth keeping, a legacy worth passing on.

And together, Gott willing, they would continue— planting and tending, building and keeping, loving and being loved, until their own final harvest came and other hands took up the work they had begun.

The door closed behind them, shutting out the cooling evening air, enclosing them in warmth and light and the sweet-smelling promise of supper. The west pasture settled into twilight peace, its blossoms folding closed for the night, its bees returning to their hives, its clover roots reaching deep into the nourished soil, holding fast against wind and weather, growing stronger in the darkness, waiting for tomorrow's sun.

THE END